Costantino Giuseppe Beschi, Grey Goosequill, Alfred Henry Forrester

Strange Surprising Adventures of the Venerable Gooroo Simple

And His Five Disciples, Noodle, Doodle, Wiseacre, Zany, and Foozle

Costantino Giuseppe Beschi, Grey Goosequill, Alfred Henry Forrester

Strange Surprising Adventures of the Venerable Gooroo Simple
And His Five Disciples, Noodle, Doodle, Wiseacre, Zany, and Foozle

ISBN/EAN: 9783744752596

Printed in Europe, USA, Canada, Australia, Japan

Cover: Foto ©Raphael Reischuk / pixelio.de

More available books at **www.hansebooks.com**

STRANGE SURPRISING ADVENTURES

OF THE VENERABLE

GOOROO SIMPLE,

AND HIS FIVE DISCIPLES,

NOODLE, DOODLE, WISEACRE, ZANY, AND FOOZLE.

Adorned with Fifty Illustrations, drawn on Wood.

BY ALFRED CROWQUILL.

LONDON:
TRÜBNER & CO., PATERNOSTER ROW.
1861.

CONTENTS.

STORY THE FIRST.

FORDING THE HISSING COBRA RIVER:

Showing how the Gooroo Simple and his Five Difciples, Noodle, Doodle, Wifeacre, Zany, and Foozle, came to a Cruel Stream, which could only be forded when it flept; together with the means they adopted to find out when it was afleep, and how they whiled away the time upon its banks by ftory-telling; Story of the Salt Merchants and the Two Affes; and ftory of the Greedy Dog and the Mutton bone; fording the River with noifelefs fteps, jala-jala and toonooko; counting heads and miffing one; and what came of it

STORY THE SECOND.

THE EGG IN THE MARE'S NEST.

STORY THE THIRD.

THE GOOROO'S RIDE ON OX-BACK.

STORY THE FOURTH.

FISHING FOR A HORSE.

STORY THE FIFTH.

THE GOOROO ON HORSEBACK.

STORY THE SIXTH.

THE PROPHECY OF POOROHITA, THE BRAHMAN.

STORY THE SEVENTH.

THE FALL FROM THE HORSE.

STORY THE EIGHTH.

THE PROPHECY FULFILLED.

LIST OF ENGRAVINGS.

THE PUBLISHERS' ADVERTISEMENT.

IT WAS a very cold, wintry day, in the middle of the dog-days of laft fummer, when it had never ceafed raining fince the fun had reached his meridian, on which, juft as we had finifhed our laft letter for the poft, our old and efteemed friend, ALFRED CROWQUILL, entered at the door of our ftore. It was evident to us that fome matter of importance muft have been the caufe of our friend's leaving the comforts of his cheerful and pleasant fireside, on such a day, for the solemn solitude of forsaken streets, and the flush and dirt of the busy city, in a pelting, pitiless storm of heavy rain. It was evident, too, from the manner in which he greeted us—with a coldness almost as chilling as the atmosphere itself on that summer's afternoon, and quite foreign to his own genial nature—that he meant to pluck a crow with us before he left our store to return home.

Reader, do you know ALFRED CROWQUILL? Of course you do; everybody does. You have bought our editions of *The Travels of Baron Munchausen,* and of the *Marvellous Adventures of Master Owl-glass,* and with these two lasting monuments of his fame in your left hand, you could not resist the impulse to cross palms with him with your right. He is already an old friend of yours, as well as of ours. All further introduction is therefore unnecessary; and you know that when he is put out——well, never mind! you know——so we at once sought to make out the why and the wherefore, or, as our friend Mr. Timbs says, "the why and because," of the apparent estrangement which was evidently spreading its upas-like tendrils round the heart of our very dear friend.

A little explanation put everything to rights. We had introduced ALFRED to another old friend of ours, GREY GOOSEQUILL, fo that the two, laying their heads together, might in due time produce this beautiful volume of *The Strange Surprifing Adventures of the Venerable Gooroo Simple*, which you are now holding fo complacently in your hand. GREY GOOSEQUILL had not furnifhed the manufeript copy with fufficient rapidity to our friend, and hence his feathers had become a little ruffled, and that was all ; and fo, when all was again calm within, though the rain ftill pattered unceafingly againft the light-reflectors of Number Sixty from without, and his own familiar fmile told that ALFRED was " himfelf again," he drew out of a myfterious recefs in the breaft of his great coat a little fquare parcel, and placed it on the table before us. It was the drawing of the Padei-yachi fniffing the Kabobs (engraved at page 91). The effect was perfectly irrefiftible ; and as it was juft our proper hour for dinner, we adjourned through the rain to the fnug room of *The Cathedral* hard by ; and, after a time, in poft-prandial talk, forgot all the annoyance of want of copy as, fafcinated by his relifh of the favoury fleam as a condiment to cold boiled rice, so graphically depicted in the face of the Padeiyachi, we enjoyed all the more the good cheer of our hoſt of *The Cathedral.*

And now, gentle reader, you will probably ask "what has all this to do with me?" Simply this : that if our book pleaſes you, your thanks are no leſs due to ALFRED CROWQUILL than our own, for having ſeduloufly laboured at the illuſtrations which adorn it, with ſo great aſſiduity that the volume has made its appearance in time to cheer up many a Chriſtmas fireſide on both ſides of the Atlantic, notwithſtanding the latenefs of the feaſon at which his many other engagements only permitted GREY GOOSEQUILL to forward the copy in a complete ſtate to our friend's transpontine ſtudio.

When the famous folio of 1623 appeared, in which, for the firſt time, "the Comedies, Hiſtories, and Tragedies of Mr. William Shakespeare" were collected together, it was accompanied by an addreſs "To the great Variety of Readers, to the moſt able, and to him that can but ſpell," by the players who gave it to the world. As we hope to number many of both theſe claſſes amongſt our patrons, we cannot do better than remind them, in the words of thoſe players, that "the fate of every Booke depends upon their capacities, and not of their heads alone, but of their purses—to read and censure it; but to buy it first, as that doth best commend a Booke, the Stationer says. Therefore, whatever you do, buy. Censure will not drive a Trade, or make the Jacke go."

And now, in the words of the printers of old, we have only to add, *Vale et nos ama*—which, for the benefit of country cousins, may be interpreted to mean, "Bye! bye! Buy!"

60, Paternoster Row,
    Christmas Eve.

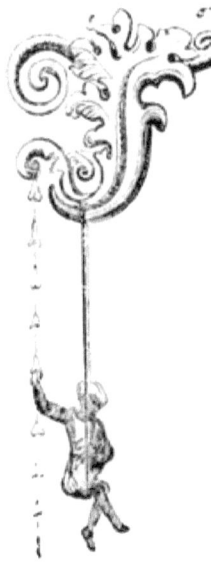

ELLING ſtories is eſſentially an Oriental accompliſhment; or, rather, if one may uſe the term, an Oriental gift, and hence it need not be wondered at that many of the tales and ſtories found in the *Geſta Romanorum*, and its kindred collections in European literature, are alſo of Oriental origin. We believe that it is now generally admitted that ſuch older tales, in which men are the perſons of the drama, are to be traced to an Eaſtern ſource; but that fables, in which animals perform the incidents and are endowed with ſpeech, properly belong to Weſtern literature. As exceptions but prove a rule, the few original fables met with in the former, and the ſtill fewer original tales of the claſs alluded to, which are found in the latter, are themſelves but evidences of the correctneſs of the theory.

It was to his education amongſt the Greeks at

B

Athens, and as the contemporary of Solon and Chilo, whofe friendfhip he enjoyed, that the young Phrygian was indebted for the elegant turn of thought and refinement of his fables, which, though illuftrating the fame human paffions and weakneffes as the tales of the Eaft, are remarkably free from the immoral allufions and coarfenefs which pervade moft of the latter. His celebrated anfwer to his friend Chilo, one of the feven fages, is at once a key to his perfonal character, and to the morality of his fables. When afked by the fage, " What God was doing?" he replied, " He is depreffing the proud and exalting the humble," an anfwer which M. Bayle, in his celebrated article on Æfop, calls truly wonderful, as proceeding from a Pagan writer who lived nearly fix centuries before the birth of Chrift.

But the elegance and refinement of the Greek fabulift were acquired at the coft of the broad humour and racinefs which form the great charm of Oriental tales, and to that humour and that racinefs was owing the popularity of the latter, which gradually fpread from Eaft to Weft, and which, till thofe Frankifh ftorytellers, Boccaccio and Chaucer, appeared in the fourteenth century, were the fources from which, with few exceptions, all our many books of ftories, once fo popular throughout Europe, had their rife.

It was owing, perhaps, to the fpread of Iflamifm through the land of the Gentoos that European literature was firft enriched with thefe fpoils from the

Eaſt ; for it was not till the tenth century that theſe Indian tales were dreſſed up in Perſian and Arabic, from which they rapidly found their way into the languages of the Weſt. Then followed, early in the thirteenth century, the empire of the Moguls, ſpreading into Europe with its power alſo the literature of the Arabs, of which theſe Indian tales then formed an eſſential portion, till gradually they at length became ſo engrafted with that of all the nations of the Weſt, changing their ſhape and colour, chameleon-like, to ſuit the taſte of each, that it is frequently difficult to trace the origin of ſome of them, which, like Proteus of old, aſſume many ſhapes and elude our graſp after all our toil, long before we can ſecure the Sanſkrit or Tamul fetters with which to bind them. In the notes ſeveral inſtances of this pliability of the rich ore will be found ; but as the object of the publiſhers was rather to furniſh an amuſing volume than a dry antiquarian treatiſe, the reader who delights in ſuch purſuits will meet with a very mine of wealth in the introductory volume to Benfey's German tranſlation of *Pantſha-tantra : five Books of Indian Fables, Tales, and Stories,* publiſhed at Leipzig in 1859.

The ſtory of the Gooroo Paramartan, of which the reader is here preſented with a free Engliſh paraphraſe, is a popular ſatire on the Brahmans, current in its detached portions in ſeveral parts of India, and has one great merit, as a whole, over moſt Hindoo compoſitions, that though by no means void of humour, and occafionally fomewhat coarfe in its allufions, none of thefe have the leaft immoral tendency.

M. Dubois, who includes a French paraphrafe of it in his *Fables et Contes Indiens*, fays that Father Befchi, who has given us a Tamul text of thefe adventures, has by some been confidered as the author and inventor of them, his intention being to turn the Brahmans and their cuftoms into ridicule; but he adds, " Mais d'après les confeignemens que j'ai été à portée d'obtenir fur ce fujet j'ai tout lieu de croire qu'il n'en fut que le compilateur. J'ai reconnu les fonds de ces contes dans des pays où ni le nom, ni les écrits du P. Befchi n'étaient jamais parvenus, et je ne fais aucun doute qu'ils ne foient réellement d'origine Indienne, au moins quant au fond, quoique ce ne foit en effet qu'une fatire fine contre les Brahmes."

Indeed, there is every probability that this fatire on the dominant cafte dates from as early a period as the ftruggles for supremacy between the Brahmans and the followers of Guadama, and is rather of Buddhift origin than an emanation from the pen of a member of the Society of Jefus; juft as when the Pope of Rome, in the Middle Ages, fent forth his fpecial police in the fhape of the mendicant friars throughout the Weftern Church,—monks and friars, Regulars and Mendicants, waged a fierce war againft each other, the principal weapon of which was fatire, traces of which we find in the roof-knots and grotefque faces, and in the carvings beneath the priefts' ftools in fo many of our ecclefiaftical edifices, and in miffal borderings and illuminations, till it found its embodiment in the poems of the followers of Wycliff, in the *Vifions of Pierce Plowman*, of Robert Langeland, and the *Canterbury Tales* of Geoffrey Chaucer.

The miffionary Befchi refided for thirty years in the South of India, and during fo long a fojourn he became thoroughly acquainted with the literature of the country, and compofed feveral Tamul works of confiderable celebrity, becoming indeed fo popular with the natives as to have received the name of *Viramamooni*, or Great Champion Devotee. He was a native of Italy, and belonged to the Propaganda Order of the Society of Jefus; was appointed by the Pope to the Eaft India Miffion, and arrived at Goa in 1700; and being fupported both by Clement XI. and Gregory XIII. he became one of the moft active miffionaries of his order, changing from time to time the field of his activity, and making himfelf mafter of the original languages and dialects of India. During a refidence at Avor, in the diftrict of Trichinopoly, he ftudied the Tamul in both its dialects,—the Koden Tamul, the ordinary dialect, and the Shen Tamul, the elegant dialect; as well as the Sanfkrit and the Teloogoo; acquiring at the fame time alfo the Hindoftannee and Perfian.

" From the moment of his arrival in India," fays Mr. Babington, " he, in conformity with Hindoo cuftom, abandoned the ufe of animal food, and employed Brahmans to prepare his meals. He adopted the habit of a religious devotee, and on his visitations to his flock assumed all the pomp and pageantry with which Hindoo Gooroos usually travel." He founded several churches, and wrote an epic upon the Madonna and Holy Family, under the title of *Tembavani*, which consists of no less than 3615 tetrasticks, and is said to possess considerable merit; and dreading apparently the kindly intentions of future critics, on the plan of the Delphin editions of the Greek and Latin classics he added a prose interpretation to each tetrastick to convey its true meaning to posterity. He composed several other works in verse, besides religious treatises of doctrine and practice, intended for the use of his converts to Christianity; and for the aid of future missionaries a Tamul and Latin Dictionary, a second in Tamul and French, and a third in Tamul and Portuguese, besides several grammars of the Koden, Tamul, and Shen Tamul, and other similar grammatical and philological works.

"M. Beschi," adds Mr. Babington, "was as much distinguished for his piety and benevolence as for his learning. To the conversion of idolaters his principal efforts were of course directed, and they are said to have been uncommonly successful. Perfect master of Hindoo science, opinions, and prejudices, he was eminently qualified to expose the fallacies of their doctrine, and the absurdities of their religious practices; and accordingly he is much extolled for the triumphs which he obtained in thofe controverfial difputations which are fo frequent among the learned in India, and for the almoft miraculous fkill which he difplayed in folving various enigmatical queftions which his adverfaries propounded for his embarraffment."

He appears gradually to have ingratiated himfelf with the native princes, rifing to the appointment of Divan, which he held under the celebrated Chunda Sahib, during his rule as Nabob of Trichinopoly, on the death of the Rajah in 1736. When the city was befieged by the Mahratta army under Morary Rao, in 1740, and Chunda Sahib taken prifoner, Befchi fled to the city of Gayal Patinam, then belonging to the Dutch, where he died, in 1742.

To Father Befchi we owe, no doubt, the collecting into one form and into the fame language the feveral tales which are here prefented to the reader; but whether he intended them to render the priefthood of the people, amongft whom he lived, ridiculous is a point upon which we feel inclined to join iffue with Mr. Babington, to whom we are indebted for the printed Tamul text, and an excellent literal tranflation of Befchi's compilation. On the contrary, confidering how perfeveringly the learned Jefuit laboured in the preparation of dictionaries and grammars of the Tamul language and dialects, we are inclined to fee in his verfion of thefe tales into Tamul little elfe than the production of a fuitable leffon-book for pupils of the Propaganda at Rome and miffionaries in India; the more fo, indeed, becaufe of the great variety of words, idiomatical expreffions and conftructions, habits and cuftoms, which he has brought together into fo fmall a compafs evidently for fuch a purpofe.

It is this latter peculiarity which makes it neceffary to prefent "The Adventures of the Gooroo Simple" to the merely Englifh reader in a free, rather than in a literal verfion, becaufe, from the great diffimilarity in the conftruction of the two languages, in the former the force and fpirit of the original would be facrificed to the mechanical rendering of the words, thus evidently employed folely for the purpofe juft ftated. This neceffity will at once be admitted, when it is known that in Tamul there is no relative pronoun, that adjectives and adverbs are mofily the fame word, and that there is alfo a conjugated derivative. The Tamul is not derived from any language that is known to us, and is probably the offspring of one now long loft, which may have ferved for the common parent of it and Teloogoo, Malayatam, and Canarefe, and date from the earlieft antiquity.

Satire is defined by Dryden to be a compofition "in which the vices and follies of mankind are inveighed againft, expofed, and held up to ridicule and contempt." It bears a near affinity to raillery, and is frequently little more than a lampoon, but always oppofed to panegyric. It muft have truth for its bafis, and however diftorted, its truthfulnefs muft ever be apparent. The narrative of the Gooroo's troubles and misfortunes is a latent attack upon the divifion into caftes of the Hindoos, the office of Gooroo being one of the higheft dignities of the higheft cafte, the members of which, from their fuppofed defcent from the mouth of Brahma, are the hereditary lights of the world, and fole expounders of the doctrines contained in the Vedas, the moft facred of Hindoo books. His five pupils, Noodle, Doodle, Wifeacre, Zany, and Foozle, may be faid to reprefent the regenerated Brahmans, receiving inftruction from the Vedas, a Brahman youth of eight to fixteen being admitted, as the cafe may be, to wear the girdle of the fecond birth, and receive that inftruction, earlier than thofe of the caftes of *Kfhatriya* and *Vaifya,* warriors and merchants, whilft the girdle is altogether denied to the *Sudra* cafte of labourers. Noodle and Doodle are both reprefented as qualifying themfelves for the higheft dignities of the Brahman cafte, denoting their pure defcent from Brahman father and mother; whilft Wifeacre, as the angler for the horfe's fhadow, may be accounted a type of the mixed cafte *Parafcara,* the fons of Brahman fathers and Sudra mothers, whofe occupation is catching fifh. Zany, in like manner, may denote a fecond mixed cafte of Brahmans, the *Mârdhâbhifhicta,* the fons of Brahman fathers and Kfhatryia mothers, whofe duty it is to teach martial exercifes; and hence, on the prefent to the Gooroo of the old worn-out horfe in the fourth ftory, he at once affumes the leaderfhip and marfhals the pro-

cesssion. So, too, in Foozle, perhaps, we are to trace
a third mixed caste of Brahmans, the *Vaidya*, the sons
of Brahman fathers and Vaisya mothers, who practise
the healing art and the cognate science of cookery, the
latter qualification in Foozle being fully set forth in the
second story. Thus we have in the *dramatis personæ*
all the chief subdivisions of the Brahmanical class
represented and ridiculed.

The literature of the Hindoos owes but little to the
hereditary claimants to the sole possession of divine
light and knowledge. On the contrary, with the
many things which the Brahmans are forbidden to
touch, if left to them alone, all science would stagnate,
and clever men, whose genius cannot be held in
trammels, therefore, soon become outcasts, and swell
the number of *Pariars* in consequence of their very
pursuit of knowledge. Thus Asangadan, the Mr.
Merriman of our tale, tells the Gooroo, in the eighth
story, that the description of the Ricebeater's Poojei,
which was evidently an emanation of his own brain,
to amuse the poor hypochondriac, will not be found
in the writings of the *Poorrachchameigans*, because to
that odious sect of Pariars in the eyes of a Brahman,
the Tamuls owe the greater part of works on science.
Then, too, we have a *Vallooran* introduced in the
fifth story, one of a sect of Pariars particularly shunned
by the Brahmans, because to them Hindoo literature
is indebted almost exclusively for the many moral
poems and books of aphorisms which are its chief

pride, ridiculing and making fun of the Gooroo and his pupils, all the time that he is duping them by a very patent impofture. Indeed, we are inclined to believe, if the conjecture ftarted with is thought untenable that thefe lampoons on the Brahmanical cafte may have emanated from the followers of Buddhifm, that, rather than to the Jefuit Father Befchi, we fhould feek to trace them to the Vallooran Pariars, whofe contempt for the arrogant and ftiff-necked ignorance of the Brahmans is thus covertly conveyed in popular ftories to the maffes of the people.

On the whole, this conjecture would appear to be fomewhat near the truth. It has already been fhown that this clafs of literature emanated chiefly from thofe defpifed outcafts, the Pariars, the very men who, ufing keener fpectacles than Dr. Robertfon, our historian of Ancient India, did (who fingularly became the panegyrift of Gentoo fubdivifions), faw that to bind human intellect and human energy within the wire-fences of Hindoo cafles is as impoffible as to fhut up the winds of heaven in a temple built by man's hand, and, throwing off their allegiance to a fyftem which fhut out all progrefs, boldly thought for themfelves. What fo likely, then, as that thefe men fhould level their fatire againft a fyftem fo fraught with mifchief to the cultivation of the intellect in its healthy connection with the world's progrefs? Accordingly, we find in the *Pantfhatantra* the fame bold attacks upon the Brahmanical cafte as thofe

which have been collected together by Father Befchi,
under the title of "The Story of the Gooroo Paramartan."

The date of the *Pantfhatantra* is not eafily afcer-
tained. Like all collections of Oriental fables and
ftories, in its feparate parts it may have exifted many
centuries before it affumed its prefent fhape and form
as a whole; or it may have gradually grown up in
its details through as many centuries, till the idea ftruck
its compiler to arrange it as we now have it. This is
fomewhat evident from the fact that the feparate
portions of the work do not form fuch a clofe and
connected illuftration of an original idea as would
have been the cafe had all the ftories belonged to one
period, or owed their origin to one mind. For our
purpofe, however, there is abundant evidence of its
exiftence prior to *Khofru Anufhirvan*, and confequently, at the clofe of the fifth or beginning of
the fixth century of the Chriftian era. *Pantfhatantra*
was made known to Europe by means of Hebrew,
Latin, and German tranflations towards the end of
the fifteenth century; fo that Befchi, living, as he
did, in the eighteenth, even if he had not been the elegant Oriental fcholar that he was, might have been
acquainted through the Latin with fome of the
materials he made ufe of in the ftory of Paramartan,
before his appointment to the Eaft India Miffion.
The original text of *Pantfhatantra* is even doubtful,
as different compilations of the ftories of which it is

compofed, under kindred titles, exift in Sanfkrit, Tamul, Canarefe, and Teloogoo; and this evidence of its great popularity in India muft abfolve Befchi from the charge of originating fo keen a fatire upon the Brahmans as are thefe "Strange Surprifing Adventures," at a time when he was eating their falt, and outwardly conforming to their habits and predilections.

By way of illuftrating the pofition we have affumed we will give two tales, taken almoft haphazard out of the fifth Tantra, pages 332—336 of the fecond volume.

"*Common fenfe is far better than book-knowledge. He who lacks common fenfe is fure to perifh, juft as it happened to the Lion-makers.*" "Pray how was that?" afked the man with the wheel. Upon which the goldmaker told the following ftory :—

The more Learned, the more Conceited and Perverse; or, the Lion-makers.

" In a certain town there once lived four Brahmans, who had the greateft affection for one another. Of thefe three had acquired all knowledge which books can impart, but poffeffed not a grain of common fenfe. The fourth had not learnt anything from books; indeed, he only had common fenfe, and nothing more. It fo happened that once they all met together to deliberate upon ' the worth of knowledge, and whether by means of it a fortune cannot be obtained by going into foreign lands and winning thereby the favour of princes?' 'At all events,' faid they, 'let us all go into foreign lands.' Accordingly, as they were journeying together, after a while, the eldeft of them faid: 'Hem! by the bye, one of us has not learnt any fcience, and only poffeffes common fenfe. Now, as princes never make gifts to the poffeffors of common fenfe without it is alfo allied to knowledge acquired from books, he muft not expect to partake of that which we fhall receive, and fo may as well at once turn back and go home again.' Upon which the fecond Brahman added: 'So ho, Mafter Common-fenfe, as you have learnt nothing, make yourfelf fcarce, and go home again!' 'No, no,' put in the third, 'to act fo would not be right and proper on our part. From childhood we have always played together, and therefore pray let him be one of us. He is a very worthy fellow, too, and as fuch fhould partake of the wealth we may acquire.' This point fettled, the four travelled on again together. By and by they came to a wood, in which were the bones of a dead lion. 'Now, then,' faid the eldeft, 'here is a fine opportunity for us to prove that knowledge is power, by bringing the dead animal again to life by means of the fciences we have acquired by deep ftudy.' Upon this one of them faid, 'I know how to put the fkeleton together;' another, 'I can produce fkin, flefh, and blood;' and the third, 'I can animate the mafs.' So the firft put the bones together into form;

the fecond added flefh, blood, and fkin; and the third was juft upon the point of animating the mafs, when he who only had common fenfe reproved him, faying, 'Why, it is a lion; if you bring him to life he will deftroy us all!' 'Fie, fie! Out upon fuch ignorance,' replied the other; 'in my hands knowledge fhall never lie idle;' upon which the other faid, 'Then wait till I firft climb up yonder tree.' When he had done this, the lion, being brought to life, fprang upon the other three and killed them; whilft he who only had common fenfe waited till the lion had departed into the jungle, when he defcended from the tree and went home unhurt."

"That is why I faid, 'Common fenfe is far better than book-knowledge; he who lacks common fenfe is fure to perifh, juft as it happened to the lion-makers.' Befides, it is alfo faid, '*They who feek wifdom only from books, without a knowledge of the ways of the world, are but learned fools, and reap the world's contempt.*'" "How is that?" afked the man with the wheel, upon which his companion told the ftory of

THE BOOK-LEARNED.

"It fo happened that there lived in a certain town four Brahmans, who were great friends. 'Hem!' faid one, 'let us go into foreign lands and acquire all fcience.' Such their determination, thefe four Brahmans fet out one day on their journey to Kanja-

kuddfha (*Kanodfha*) to become perfect mafters of
fcience.   Arrived at their deftination, they entered a
mattam under a celebrated Gooroo, and ftudied dili-
gently.   Here they remained for twelve years, during
which time, as they only occupied their minds with
their books, they acquired all knowledge which books
can impart.   Upon this, they all four met together
and faid, ' We have fuccefsfully croffed the ftream of
knowledge ; now, therefore, let us afk permiflion of
the wife Gooroo to depart and return again to our
homes.'   When all had repeated, ' So let it be,' they
begged of the Gooroo to allow them to depart, and
having obtained his permiflion, they packed up their
books and ftarted for home.   After a while they came
to a part of the road where it divaricated to the right
and to the left; fo having feated themfelves by the
wayfide, ' Now,' afked one, ' which way are we to go ?'

  * * * * * *

 " Some time after, as thefe learned Brahmans were
purfuing their way in the company of a pilgrim
journeying to a meeting of pious devotees, they came
to a grave-yard, in which there was a donkey cropping
the rank herbage from the graves.   So they all at once
began to afk, ' What is that ?' and one of them opening his book,* as is their wont, and applying the firft

---

* Thefe *Sortes* are of very early origin, and were no doubt adopted
from the Eaft by the Greeks, and Sir Richard Paul Jodrell, in his
" Illuftrations of Euripides" (vol. i., p. 174), informs us that a fimilar
practice prevailed amongft the Hebrews, by whom it was called *Bath-*

paffage which meets the eye to the exigences of the
cafe, read aloud, 'He who ftands is of thy kindred,'
upon which he faid, 'This, then, is one of us;' whereupon they all came around the afs, one kiffing him, and
another fhaking him by the fore foot. Whilft so
engaged, they alfo efpied a camel. 'What, then, is
that?' afked they. So the third opened his book and
read, 'Swift is the courfe of Dharma.'* 'Surely,
then,' faid he, 'that is Dharma;' upon which the
fecond added, 'Love fhould lead to Dharma;' faying
which he took the afs and tied it to the neck of the
camel. This was feen by a paffer-by, who went and
told the Valkeer who owned the donkey, and who fet
off immediately, intending to give the learned blockheads a found thrafhing; but they, feeing him running
towards them, made off as faft as their legs would
carry them.

After a while they came up to a river, which they
had to crofs, when one of them, feeing a palm leaf
floating down the ftream, faid, 'That which floats
will carry us over,' and immediately jumping upon it,
went down and only fhowed his head above the

---

kol. Every one will recollect the allufion made by Gibbon to it (vol. vi.
p. 333) where the meffengers of Clovis are reprefented as liftening to the
words of the pfalm being chanted as they enter the fhrine of St. Martin,
and alfo the prophecy of evil to Charles the Firft from an application of
the *Sortes Virgiliana*, when he opened upon *Æneidos*, lib. iv. vers. 615,
&c. The early Chriftians ufed the Bible for the fame purpofe till it was
put down by the authority of the Church.

* Juftice; alfo the God of Juftice and of Death.

water. Seeing this, one of his companions feized him by the hair of his head, and, exclaiming, 'When a lofs of the whole is threatened, a wife man will be content to preferve a part; to lofe all is hard indeed,' he cut off the head of the drowning man.

"The three others proceeded on their journey, and came, about the firft watch of the night, to a village, three inhabitants of which afked each one of the Brahmans to be his gueft, and took him to his houfe, fo that thefe learned men were feparated for the time in three different dwellings. By way of refrefhment, before one was placed fome vermicelli, prepared with fugar and butter; fo, opening his book, he read,—'He who takes long threads comes to an end,' upon which he turned on his heel, and left the food untafted. The hoft of the fecond placed paftry with whipped cream before him; but remembering the faying,—'What is too thin and too big will not live long,' he too departed without touching the food prepared for him. The third, to whom fome buttered crumpets were prefented, turned to his book, and read,—'Where there are holes, there evil lurks,' fo he, too, went his way. In this manner, then, did thefe three book-learned blockheads travel on, weary, hungry, and thirfty, to their home, laughed at by the villagers, and defpifed for their want of common fenfe, and it was this which made me fay,—'*They who feek wifdom only from books, without a knowledge* of the ways of the world, are but learned fools, and reap the world's contempt.' "

The only trait of Brahman cleverneſs which the tale of the Gooroo portrays is the cunning way in which, in the ſixth ſtory, the *Poorahita* gets out of a dilemma by the aſſumption of a knowledge which he did not poſſeſs, ſimply by uttering the myſtical jargon :—

ASANAM · SHITAM · JIVANA · NASHAM.

THE STRANGE SURPRISING ADVENTURES OF THE VENERABLE GOOROO SIMPLE.

THE FIRST STORY.

FORDING THE HISSING COBRA RIVER:

Showing how the Gooroo Simple and his Five Difciples, Noodle, Doodle, Wifeacre, Zany, and Foozle, came to a Cruel Stream, which could only be forded when it flept; together with the means they adopted to find out when it was afleep, and how they whiled away the time upon its banks by ftory-telling; Story of the Salt Merchants and the Two Affes; and ftory of the Greedy Dog and the Mutton bone; fording the River with noifelefs fteps; jala-jala and toonooko; counting heads and mifling one; and what came of it.

NCE upon a time, there lived in the land of the Hindoos a holy Gooroo, whofe facred calling, no lefs than his wondrous wifdom, led all men to reverence him. He had five followers, or difciples, who attended his fteps, aiding him in his duties, and honouring and serving him; sharing his boiled rice as their daily food, and picking up the golden words of wisdom which fell from his lips, as pearls beyond all price, to be treasured up for ever. The chief of these disciples was named Noodle, and came from a very long line of ancestors, his pedigree being only lost in the Flood. Then came Doodle, a wise youth, who loved to lie under the shade of the trees, which surrounded the mattam of the Gooroo, in which they all lived, and with closed eyes, to watch the motion of the clouds in order to study the theory and cause of rain. Next was Wiseacre, the good Gooroo's right-hand man, whom he delighted to honour, and to employ upon all important occasions, even to the purchase of a horse. After him came Foozle and Zany, two youths of very different characters, but both of great promise; and though neither of them had the aptitude of Noodle, the deep thought of Doodle, nor the promptitude of Wiseacre, it seldom happened but that, after much and mature consideration, both Foozle and Zany became of the same mind in all things with the Gooroo and his three more promising disciples.

One day the Gooroo and his five pupils had made the visitation of his district, teaching the people as they went along, and increasing the number of his disciples, when, all at once, about midday, just at the third watch, the whole six found themselves on the bank of a stream, which they had to ford on their way home to the mattam, the white pinnacles of which they could fee ftanding out in the funlight from amongft the far diftant trees. After a little fearch to difcover where this could beft be managed, they came to a fhelving flope in the bank, and juft as Zany and Noodle, Doodle, Foozle, and Wifeacre, were about to ftep into the water, the thoughtful Gooroo ftayed them in thefe words :—

"My children, let us act with caution. This River is, at beft, an ill-conditioned and fpiteful one, and not a few are the tales told of its treachery and cunning, of the heavy difafters which have befallen travellers who trufted to its good faith, and the defolation it has fpread over many a happy home. Now, I have heard that it is never fafe to intruft one's felf to it while it is awake, but only when it is afleep; fo that it is always wife, before venturing to put one's foot in it, firft to afcertain whether it is awake or not. Therefore, Wifeacre, my fon, do thou approach noifeleffly on tiptoe to its margin, and find out whether it has yet turned in for its noonday reft, and has gone to fleep. That done, we fhall be able to act with prudence, and decide whether to crofs at once, or wait for a more aufpicious moment."

All admired the wifdom and forethought of their mafter, and Wifeacre, by way of preparation for fo important a duty, lighted a cheroot, and approached daintily and gingerly on tiptoe, as he had been told, the margin of the treacherous River, carrying with him the burning brand, which had ferved him to light

his "weed," though he now could fcarcely hold the
cheroot between his teeth, fo anxious had he become.
When he had got within arm's-length of the ftream,
he ftretched out his hand as he bent forward to the
utmoft, and touched the water with the lighted brand,
when the River immediately fent forth a hiffing noife,
like a ferpent about to encompafs its prey.   In his
fright, Wifeacre fcarcely made two bounds ere he

reached the top of the bank, where the Gooroo and
his fellow pupils were feated.   "O, Mafter, Mafter!"
faid he, when he had recovered his breath, "the perfidious River is wide awake!   This is, indeed, no time
for fording it; for no fooner had I touched it, than it
flew into a rage, and, hiffing like a fnake, would have
worried and fwallowed me up, if I had not rufhed

away; and, of a truth, I fcarcely know how I got
here; for, in its anger at my intrufion, it fputtered and
fmoked, and leaped, and rufhed at me as I bounded
up the bank. Indeed, indeed, Mafter! your wifdom
and caution have faved us; for, had we ventured to
crofs the River without firft afcertaining if it were
afleep or no, not one of us would have been left to
tell the tale, fo angry and fierce was its wrath."

It is pleafant to all men to feel that the advice we
give to one another has been found and good, and to
one fo wife and learned as the Gooroo it was now particularly fo. So, when Wifeacre had finifhed the report
of his efcape from his incenfed enemy, to which all
had liftened with painful attention and aftonifhment,
the Gooroo looked down benignly upon the affembled
group of pupils, faying—"No *wife* man counfels
another to act at variance with the will of the gods."
He had pronounced thefe words in the folemn tone
in which he was in the habit of addreffing the flock of
his diocefe, and had fkilfully put the emphafis on the
word *wife*. It had its effect; for, from long experience
Noodle, Doodle, and Wifeacre well knew that now
would follow words of true wifdom, fuch as few other
men could utter. After a fhort paufe he continued—
"My children, may the will of the gods and our
deftiny be propitious! To the firft we muft bow; to
the fecond we muft fubmit! What is ordained for
him will fall to the lot of man. Even the gods cannot
hinder it. Therefore, do not let us repine at fate, but
wonder; for that which is ours belongs to none other.

If contradictions and calamities befet our path in life, by patience and refignation we muft ftrive to reconcile the one and to bear the other. Follow me, therefore, to the fhade of yonder palms, and there patiently, and with proper fubmiffion to our fate, let us abide for a while and watch for a more favourable opportunity."

Having feated themfelves around their honoured mafter, in order that the time might not hang heavily upon his hands, and to divert him from thinking inwardly with clofed eyes, abftracted for the time from this paffing world and its troubles, as in fuch moments of leifure he was often wont, his difciples fought to intereft him by repeating to him fuch tales refpecting the River, then the great object of their anxiety, as had come to the knowledge of any one of them. Noodle, as the eldeft of them, thus began :—

"When my grandfather was ftill alive, and I was yet but a little child, he would fet me on his knee, and, as from the window of the houfeplace we could fee this River reflecting the light of the fky amongft the palm trees, which grow upon its banks, he would often tell me inftances of its deceit and cruelty. One in particular I well recollect; for many a time and oft did he repeat it, as he himfelf was the fufferer by the dodges of the fwindling ftream. You are aware that my grandfather was a merchant well known in this country, and that the chief article which he dealt in was falt. One day, accompanied by a fellow-trader, each of them leading an afs laden with two bags of falt, they had to crofs the ftream fomewhere about the very fpot where Wifeacre met with his adventure but now. There had been a heavy fall of rain on the previous night, and the River was much fwollen, fo that the bags of falt reached down into the water; but, mark you, there was no hole in the bags, which were each fecurely faftened at the mouth with a ftrong leather thong, fo that the falt could not drop out of itfelf.

"The day was very hot, and the coolnefs of the water was pleafant to the travellers and their beafts; fo that they were in no hurry to crofs the River, but loitered for a long while on the paffage, whilft the water fcarcely rofe up to their middle even in the deepeft places. The affes, too, enjoyed the refrefhing bath as much as their mafters; and, as there was a long journey before them, my grandfather thought it would greatly refrefh the beafts if they were allowed the fame indulgence as himfelf and companion. At length, however, it was neceffary to quit the ftream and purfue their journey.

"Upon arriving at the oppofite bank, judge of their aftonifhment to find, that though the leather thongs had certainly never been tampered with, the four bags, which they themfelves had filled to the brim with falt, and even preffed down with heavy weights to make them hold the more, were now quite empty, not a fingle grain of falt being left in either of them! And, more wonderful ftill, this had all happened fo noifeleffly, that neither my grandfather nor the other merchant had heard the leaft found, whilft the River was ftealing the falt, so they foon convinced themfelves that it had been done by magic; elfe, how, without making a rent in the bags, or untying the leather thongs which faftened their mouths, had the falt been all fo cleverly filched away? Therefore, feeing that they and their beafts had efcaped with their lives out of the clutches of fuch a great and powerful enemy, they were thankful to the gods that, in its greedy hafte to fpoil them of their merchandife, the River had given them fufficient time to make their own efcape with no greater lofs than the whole of their ftock in trade."

Doodle, who, during the time that Noodle was narrating this fingular and furprifing adventure of his grandfather and the other merchant, had been lying on his back, with clofed eyes, fo that nothing fhould diftract his attention from it, now raifed himfelf up, faying: " I, too, have heard many tales of the cheats and dodges of this River. Indeed, they are in everybody's mouth in this part of the country, fo many and various have been its wiles; but one that has been the fubject of much difcuffion, both at home and abroad, is that which, with our dear mafter's permiffion, I will now narrate.

" I forget when it happened; but as I myfelf have feen it in a very old book, I may as well fay, a long time ago a farmer, having killed a fheep and jointed it, hung the joints up in an outhoufe, leaving the windows open to allow a current of air to pafs through the building to keep the meat from turning bad, as the weather was then very hot. About the farm, amongſt others, was a cunning old dog, who, though well enough fed and cared for by the farmer and his ſons, was not often indulged with a feaſt off the beſt joints brought to his maſter's table; and, if he had a weakneſs, it was certainly a love of good living. Dogs, as well as men, are luxurious animals, and, like their maſters, they have their moments of temptation. There was the open window; there, too, was the mutton beyond. The long and the ſhort of it is, the temptation was too great; and, in lefs time than it takes me to tell it, the dog was feen ſtealthily approaching the River with as pretty a ſhoulder of mutton in his mouth as ever graced the table of that great monarch of the Weſt, whoſe favourite diſh was a cold ſhoulder in its virgin ſtate from the ſpit of the previous day, with which cold ſhoulder, since that day, many people delight to enter-tain their viſitors.

" Effectually to hide his theft, the cunning old dog knew it would be both wife and prudent to crofs the River and enjoy his meal on the oppoſite bank, where, too, he could bury the bone more ſecurely from the many dogs which were kept on the farm. 'Stolen pleaſures are ſweeteſt,' said he to himſelf, as he entered the water. Was it the echo of his mut-tered thought that ſeemed to come from the bottom of the ſtream? He could not help looking down to fee from whence the found came. Sure enough, there he faw another dog, and with fuch a dainty

ſhoulder of mutton in his mouth, the fat ſo white,
and the lean ſo red, and, better than all, ſo much
larger than his own! Now, the farmer's dog, though
old and cunning, had ſtill plenty of pluck, and did
not fear to match himſelf with any dog of his own
ſize and ſtrength. Beſides, he would have his adver-
ſary at an advantage; for the latter could not bite as
long as he held the mutton in his mouth, and if he
dropped it, as it was the mutton he cared for and

not the dog, he could eaſily ſnap it up, and carry it
off as the ſpoil of the fight. He uttered a growl and
ſhowed his teeth, plunging at the ſame time down
into the water to ſeize the tempting prey; but there
was neither dog nor ſhoulder of mutton there; and,
whilſt ſo engaged, the River had carried that away
which, but a moment before, he had held in his own

mouth; so the dog lost his dinner, and the cheat of a River it must have been that had muttered, 'Stolen pleasures are sweetest,' to make the dog lose his substance for the shadow."

As Doodle uttered these words, Zany and Foozle, who had not paid much attention to what he was saying, had been watching a horseman in the distance, who now advanced rapidly from the opposite bank, and as he saw that the water was little more than a foot deep, he dashed into it, and without hesitation crossed the stream with rapidity and ease. "Would that our dear master had a horse," said Foozle, "for then both he and we might, all in turn, cross the River without any fear, as quickly and pleasantly as did yonder horseman." "Would that our dear master had a horse," repeated Zany, and "would that our dear master had a horse," re-echoed Doodle, Wiseacre, and Noodle; saying which the whole five surrounded the Gooroo, entreating him to buy a horse as soon as he had an opportunity, and to never mind the damages.

The Gooroo approved of their advice; but as the shades of evening were already closing around them, and he had no inclination to spend the night supperless where they then were, he thus addressed them: "Thanks, my children, for this expression of your loving care for my comfort; but as the purchase of a horse is a matter which demands much and serious consideration, we will talk it over upon some future

occafion. At prefent our firft care muft be to crofs
the River, or we fhall not reach the mattam to-night,
and to camp out till morning will not be over pleafant ;
fo Noodle had better go at once and afcertain whether
the River is gone to fleep at laft."

Noodle, taking a leaf out of Wifeacre's book, deter-
mined to proceed with great caution. Accordingly,
holding the extinguifhed brand in his right hand, he
ftretched himfelf upon all-fours, and crept noifeleffly
to the margin of the ftream, where, at arm's-length,
he immerfed the fame end of the ftick which the
River had extinguifhed upon Wifeacre's firft vifit, and
watched the refult with trembling anxiety. This time
there was no hiffing nor fputtering, no fmoke nor
noife, fave only the found of a gentle ripple as the
ftick broke the current of the ftream, like the foft
breathing of a fleeping beauty. Noodle filently with-
drew the brand ; but knowing full well, from his
grandfather's experience with the bags of falt, that the
River's quiet might only be a fham, more fecurely to
entrap its prey, he again immerfed the ftick till it
ftruck the bed of the ftream. All was quiet as before ;
and now, certain that the River was really faft afleep,
he raifed himfelf noifeleffly up, and walking with a
ftealthy ftep towards the Gooroo, with a face radiant
with joy he exclaimed, " Mafter, dear mafter ! Now
is the time to crofs the River ; there is no longer need
of fear or alarm. The time of its deep flumber is
come ; let us then pafs over to the other fide quickly

and noiselessly, not uttering a single word till we are safely out of its clutches."

The Gooroo, and Foozle, and Doodle, Wiseacre, and Zany, no sooner heard the good news than they one and all rose to their feet at once, in order to steal a march upon the sleeping stream; but even under the excitement of such a moment his pupils did not fail to remember the respect due to their master, whose followers they were, and would insist that he should have the post of honour and precedence; whilst the Gooroo, on the contrary, in his great love and affection for his children, would have willingly been the last to enter the River, that so he might have been on dry land till the others had done so, ready to render assistance should either of them unexpectedly cause the enemy suddenly to waken up and assume a hostile position. This point had to be discussed by signs, for no one dared to utter a single word; and whether it was so intended, or whether the Gooroo only wished to indicate his desire that Zany, who was the youngest, should be the first to enter, the old chronicler has omitted to relate, and his erudite editor, the great Champion-devotee, Viramamooni, is equally silent on the subject. All we know is, that, taking the extinguished brand out of the hand of Noodle, he pointed with it towards Zany, and that, in doing so, as Zany stood the furthest off in the line of pupils preparing for their descent into the River, the action seemed to indicate his wish that all should proceed in

a straight line, keeping step like soldiers, and thus cross
the stream.

"Without uttering a single word," says Viramamooni, " all six of them cautiously descended into the
water, which reached up to their knees, whilst their
hearts beat time audibly as they placed first the right
and then the left foot, *jala-jala*, alternately so stealthily
in the stream, that in pressing each down to the

River's bed, they touched it, *toonookoo*, so noiselessly
that the sleeper was not disturbed, and even the
coverlid, which the water formed, made no rippling
ound." Caution and prudence were qualities pre-
eminently marked by large bumps in the skull of the
Gooroo, and never was there an occasion more fitted
for their display than the present, though the short
steps thus necessitated made the passage long.

But, notwithſtanding all this caution, a miſchance happened which no one could have calculated upon. Arrived on the oppoſite bank, they began to ſhout and cut the moſt fantaſtic capers for very joy, till, all of a ſudden it occurred to Wiſeacre to count and ſee if all had reached land ſafely; but, count as he would, he could only make out five inſtead of the ſix, who had entered the River. There was the Gooroo; and Noodle, and Doodle, and Zany, and Foozle, were alſo

there; but where was the ſixth? To make himſelf the more ſure that one was miſſing, he begged that they would all ſtand apart in a ſtraight line, and, beginning with Foozle and Zany, then on to Doodle and Noodle, he came at laſt to the Gooroo, but always with the ſame reſult—one out of the ſix was miſſing. Full of his diſcovery, Wiſeacre then ſaid: "Hem, and alack-a-day! Woe is me! Woe is me!

We went fix into the stream, and five only have come out! The cruel, treacherous River has swallowed up one of us! Behold, Master! count yourself: there are but five of us here!" Again the Gooroo ranged them all in a row, and beginning with Wiseacre, he told off each respectively on his fingers: Wiseacre, Noodle, Doodle, Zany, and Foozle: and though he counted them thus some half-dozen times, he could only make the number five instead of fix. With a like result Noodle, Doodle, Zany, and Foozle attempted to count the number. Certain it was, fix went in, and five came out; for none of them could make the number more, and one, therefore, was unquestionably drowned. Satisfied that fuch was the cafe, they rent the air with their lamentations, and, embracing one another, they one and all exclaimed, " Heaven be praised that we five, who stand here, have escaped! O, cruel, cruel River! Perfidious wretch that thou art, more sanguinary than a bear, a wolf, or a tiger, who hast dared to swallow up one of the disciples of the great and good Gooroo Simple! Would nothing less satisfy thee, than to make a supper off one of the pupils of that great and venerated faint, whose name is reverenced throughout the land? Who will henceforth venture to touch thy treacherous billows with the sole of his foot, now that thou hast consummated fuch an act of perfidy towards one whom all the world delights to honour?

" Cursed be thou in thy generation! May thy

fource be dried up and perifh ! thy bed become arid,
and thy waves be confumed by fire ! Without moift-
ure, without coolnefs, without a record of the fpot of
thy prefent exifience, mayft thou vanifh from the face
of the earth, and thy very afhes be fcattered to the
winds !"

Thus venting their rage, and interlacing the fingers
of their hands in order to produce the found of cracking of the joints as they projected them forwards, to
add folemnity to their maledictions, they wound up
the whole by fhowering down upon the River hand-
fuls of duft till the clear ftream became a muddy pud-
dle, becaufe, in fo doing, they knew that their imprecations were ftrengthened in the fight of the gods.

In all their lamentations and imprecations, no one
of them mentioned the name of him that was mifling ;
for, as each had omitted to count himfelf when telling off the others on his fingers, no one could name
the one whofe death they were lamenting, feeing that
each had mifled himfelf alone, and every one was thus
grieving for his own lofs and not for the lofs of a
companion, without knowing it.

Juft as they were cafting the laft volley of duft into
the ftream, and fcreaming out a final curfe, a traveller
approached the fpot upon which they were ftanding,
and addreffed himfelf to them in thefe words : " How
now, firs ! What's the row ? Who's dead ? and
what's to pay ?"

" Who's dead ?" reiterated the Gooroo ; " who's

dead? who can tell? who can know? Careful and
cautious as we have been, knowing its wiles and mif-
trufting appearances, the accurfed River has fwallowed
up one of us; for fix of us walked down into the
ftream, and fee, count as you will, there are only five
of us now on dry land!" Then Noodle related how
they had watched for the River's going to bed for
many long hours on the oppofite bank; how Wifeacre had nearly become a facrifice to its perfidy in the
morning; and how he himfelf had been cheated into
the belief that it was abed and afleep, of which the
artful creature only put on the femblance to lull fuf-
picion, and the more fecurely to rob the good Gooroo
of one of his difciples. Then he told the traveller
how his grandfather had been robbed of his falt, and
called upon Doodle to repeat how the fhoulder of
mutton had been filched by the big cheat of a River,
even out of the very mouth of the dog, who was
crofling; but the traveller ftopped him fhort, by faying, 'Enough! enough! I have heard that ftory
long ago, when I was a boy; and I believe every boy
can fay the fame thing. The fact is, no one fhould
crofs this wicked ftream without firft fecuring fuch a
magic ftaff as that which I now hold in my hand, by
means of which he would then pafs over fafely, and never
allow himfelf to be drawn down out of his depth into
the bed of the River. However, what's done is done,
and can't be undone. The longer the faw of grief is
drawn, the hotter it grows! It's no ufe sitting ftill

under a calamity, for the gods help only those who help themselves, and it seems as if they have sent you the means, if you employ them properly. I am well versed in magic arts, have read the stars, and am intimate with all the planets. People call me Zadjeet, because of the wonderful things I have foretold, and the wonderful things I have done; but I cannot rule the planets, nor consult the stars, unless my palm is crossed with the precious metals, because, you must know, the lines of my hands form the magic sentence, ' *Fo ol sand the irm one ya reso onpar ted,*' by which, under such circumstances, I am forced to act. Now, I can restore him whom ye mourn; but if I do so, what shall be my recompense ?"

To this the Gooroo replied, unfastening the belt which he wore round his waist, " In this girdle are forty and five fanams, all that remain of the sum set apart for our journey, of which this has been but the first day."

" *Fo ol sand the irm one ya reso onpar ted,*" said the magician. " 'Tis but a scurvy sum for the restoration to you of one whose death you are mourning; but because all the world honours the Gooroo Simple, I, too, will show my veneration and respect for such profound wisdom as his, and cause all six persons to stand here and respond to my call. This magic staff," he continued, holding up his walking-cane in front of the Gooroo, " is the agency by which this will be brought about. Stand, all of you, in a line, and close

your eyes, leſt evil ſhould befal any one as puniſhment
for peeping. When you hear each one alternately
give his name, in reply to my queſtion, count off the
number on your fingers till the whole ſix have re-
ſponded." No ſooner was the line formed, with the
Gooroo at one end and Wiſeacre at the other, than
the magician, raiſing his cane, let it fall with a heavy
thwack upon the ſhoulders of the Gooroo, crying out,
at the ſame time, "Who is this? who is this?"

"Enough! enough!" replied the Gooroo. "It is
I myſelf, the Gooroo Simple."—"Score one," ſaid
the magician; and bringing his cane to bear, with a
ſharp cut, acroſs the ſhoulders of Noodle, "Who is
this?" he aſked.—"Mercy, mercy! 'tis I, Noodle."

—" Score two," put in the wonderful Zadjeet, as he let fall a heavy blow on the left fhoulder of Doodle, afking, at the fame time, " Who is this?"—" Doodle, Doodle, Doo——."—" Score three," faid the magician," ftopping him fhort, and bringing his cane down, with a heavy blow, upon the rounded back of Foozle (who had bent his head downwards when he clofed his eyes), repeating, at the fame time, his queftion of " Who is this?"—" Oh, oh! Foozle,

Foozle!"—" Score four," was the curt rejoinder, as the cane fell upon the fhoulders of Zany with a hearty thwack, and the queftion of " Who is this?" was repeated.—" Don't, don't! Oh, oh! Zany, Zany!" was the reply.—" Score five; one, two, three, four, five," faid the magician, as he gave Wifeacre fome half-dozen telling hits, both right and left, again repeating, for the laſt time, " Who is this?"—" Oh, me! oh, me! 'tis I, Wifeacre, the difciple of the wife Gooro Simple."—" Score fix," was Zadjeet's reply. " He is the loft one reſtored to you; and now I may fairly claim my reward."

" Wonderful magician!" faid the Gooroo. " Wonderful magician!" repeated each difciple, rubbing his back the while; " wonderful magician!" Satisſied that the loft one was found, and that now not one of the fix was miſſing, the Gooroo handed over his girdle with the forty-five fanams to Zadjeet, the magician, whofe eyes twinkled as, chuckling, he went away, humming to himfelf, " *Fo ol ſand the irm one ya reſo onpar ted,*" whilſt the Gooro Simple, Noodle, Doodle, Wifeacre, Zany, and Foozle, continued their homeward journey to the mattam.

STORY THE SECOND.

THE EGG IN THE MARE'S NEST.

The old crone of the Mattam teaches them how to count nofes; the neceflity for horfe-flefh quite a Parliamentary difcuffion; difcovery of a Mare's Neft; thoughts on Incubation; the duties of the Mattam; felecting the Egg; the Foal and its gambols; lofs of the Foal, and what it led to.

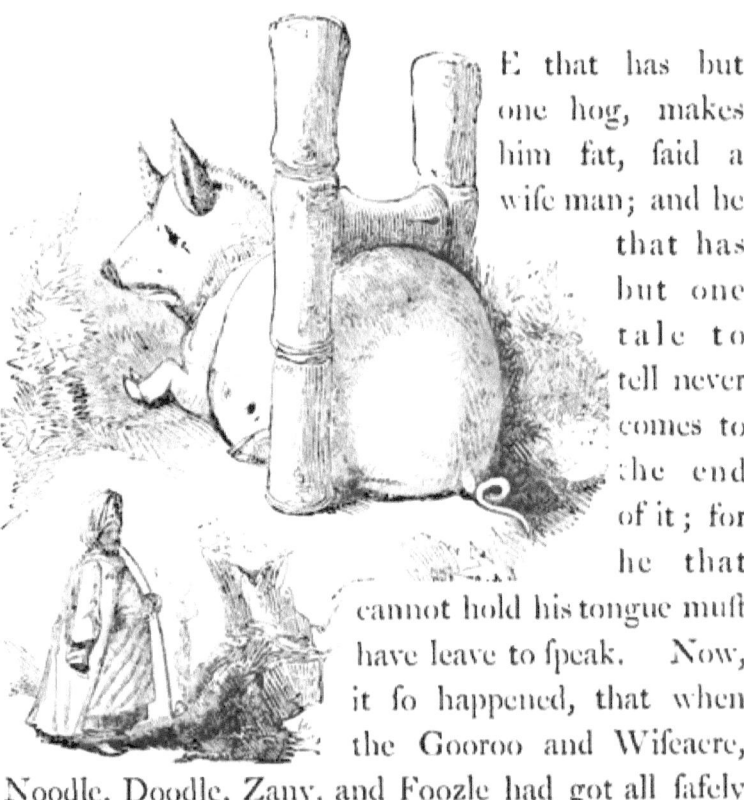

E that has but one hog, makes him fat, faid a wife man; and he that has but one tale to tell never comes to the end of it; for he that cannot hold his tongue muft have leave to fpeak. Now, it fo happened, that when the Gooroo and Wifeacre, Noodle, Doodle, Zany, and Foozle had got all fafely within the walls of the mattam, they firft began to

compare notes amongst themselves of the day's adventures, and the dangers overcome in the passage of
the River; and it was not until this had been done
over and over again, that each became more fully
aware how great had been those dangers, and with
what heroic fortitude they had been met and overcome. Each felt himself to be a hero, and in the
East, no less than in the West, it has long been the
fashion for heroes to tell their own tales, and to tell
them in their own way, with small fear of contradic-
tion from their listeners. The Gooroo, as was his
wont, improved the occasion, and as it is written,
"like lips like lettuce," so did each of his pupils
also. One heard of nothing but the River and his
dodges; of Zadjeet and the recovery of number six;
till at last, as the stomach will not relish partridges
every day for dinner, and the ear loves variety no less,
the River began to stink in men's nostrils, as if the
drainage of some dirty city had been its enforced
daily diet, without stint or limit, ever since the good
Gooroo had put his foot in it.

Now it so happened that there was living at the
mattam an old crone, blind of one eye, but with a
tongue that made ample amends for that deficiency.
It was her office to clean out the mattam, and to
wash the sacred precincts with a fluid rendered more
precious by the addition of that which had passed
through the cow's stomach, and which it was her
daily duty to collect for the purpose, as the fragrant

odour which it imparted was typical of the fanctity of the place. So when this old woman heard fo much about the wonderful efcape of her mafter and his difciples, and about nothing elfe, fhe determined to pay them in their own coin, and fo take them down a peg.

"To be plain with you," faid fhe, one morning, whilft engaged in her important duty, when the whole group were ftanding by, to inhale the rich perfume, "I cannot help thinking your method of counting heads would never have yielded the right fum; for it appears to me that each, in taking stock of the whole, did what very few other people do—lost sight of number one. However, if such an occasion should again occur, I will tell you of a surer method to arrive at the truth, and one which, fifty years ago, proved most satisfactory to those who adopted it. You must know there was a great festival and merry-making going on in one of the neighbouring villages at the time, and, in company with a lot of other girls of our own age, my sister and I had journeyed thither. As girls will do, we had been up to all kinds of Mag's-diversions by the way, running here and there, and playing at hide-and-seek; so she who was leader—and a right merry and wise creature she was too—said, 'Let us count noses, and see that we are all here, before we enter the village; and the best way, and the surest, to do that is, to kneel down in a ring, and each dip her nose into the circlet which the cow has just dropped here, when I can readily see if any are wanting, by counting up the impressions so made.' We were some *ten* or so when we started, so we did as she bid us, and when we rose to our feet again, she counted over the impressions, and finding them just as many again as half, she knew that we were all there and none missing, as sure as the two halves always make the whole."

The Gooroo and his disciples, who did not perceive that the old crone was poking fun at them by giving a definite idea to an indefinite number, could not but admire the advice fhe gave, and promifed to follow it, if there fhould be again a neceffity for counting nofes. "It is a pity," faid Wifeacre, "that we did not know of it before, becaufe it cofts neither money nor ftripes to folve the problem; and the lofs of the one is often more hard to bear than the fmart of the other. Still, all things confidered, it will be beft to buy a horfe. Indeed, fir, you muft get a horfe!" When Wifeacre had faid this, Noodle and Doodle, Zany and Foozle, all chimed in, "Indeed, fir, you muft buy a horfe!" upon which Wifeacre proceeded, "It is the only fure way to avert fuch calamities for the future, as we ourfelves have experienced by the River; fo never mind the coft, fir, but get a horfe."

Like many a wife man in other ftations of life, the Gooroo could no longer withftand the preffure from without, and fo, if only to gain time, if not to fhelve the fubject altogether, he appeared to give in to their wifhes, defiring, however, as a preliminary ftep, to know what a horfe would coft? None could tell, and fo feveral days were gained by the Gooroo, in the time it took to make the neceffary inquiries, draw up the report, and difcufs it after a day had been fet apart for the purpofe at a previous meeting; becaufe fo grave a matter as the purchafe of a horfe did not admit of the omiffion of any of the forms which the Gooroo and his difciples adopted when they had to make rules for the guidance of the diftrict over which he prefided, and of which the mattam, in which he dwelt, formed the council-houfe. At length the important day arrived; the report was read and difcuffed by the five difciples in the outer court, and approved; fo Wifeacre was deputed to take it into the room in which the Gooroo fat in ftate to tranfact bufinefs, where he placed it on the table and retired, bowing reverently to his mafter as he left his prefence. The Gooroo would willingly have let it lie on the table, whence, in due courfe, it would have been claimed as a perquifite by the old crone who fwept out the mattam; but he could not treat with fo marked a difrefpect a document which had been unanimoufly approved of by all his difciples, fo he pleaded many and more preffing engagements at firft, then the neceffity of keeping it a week for deliberation; and when, at laft, he could find no more excufes, he put on a bold face, and fent for Noodle, Wifeacre, Doodle, Foozle, and Zany, and bidding them fit down, he read the report aloud, till he came to the words, "A good horfe will coft at the leaft fifty to one hundred pagodas;" faying which, he flung the report upon the floor, and, trampling upon it with both his feet, he exclaimed, "A hundred pagodas! Do you dare to pafs your jokes upon me? Where's the money to come from, I fhould like to know? And, if I had it, I would not buy a horfe at that price. No, no; my legs have carried me hitherto, and will do fo ftill. Begone; and let no one dare again to talk to me about buying a horfe for a hundred pagodas!" So the matter dropped; for after he had snubbed them fo, who would dare to mention it again?

Now Wifeacre had many commiffions to execute for his mafter, and did not at all like the idea of giving up the purchafe of the horfe, as he knew very well when he had to go to diftant villages, as was often the cafe, the horfe would be as much his as his mafter's, if he only could get the latter to pay for it. And chance now feemed to come to his aid. One evening the cow which fupplied them with milk did not return to the mattam from its pafturage, fo all five difciples went out in the village to make diligent fearch for her; but meeting with no fuccefs, it was determined that Wifeacre fhould make the tour of the furrounding villages for a like purpofe. After three days' ineffectual fearch he returned to the mattam, and any one who knew his ways, faw at once that Wifeacre had fomething important to communicate. The Gooroo, who had miffed the delicious milk of the cow for three days, immediately reverted to her lofs as the fubject uppermoft in his mind, and afked, before Wifeacre had time to open his mouth, "Where's the cow? have you found her, and brought her back?"

"The cow, fir? Never mind the cow, fir! I could gain no tidings of her, fearch as I would; but, what is far better than the cow, fir, I have met with a thorough-bred horfe dog-cheap, and fuch a bargain

E

as may never occur again." All drew eagerly round
the fpeaker, and the Gooroo, evidently delighted at
getting a horfe at the price of a dog, faid, " How is
that, my fon ? Where has this piece of good fortune
turned up? Give us all the particulars, that we may
lofe no time in fecuring the good the gods have fent
us."

" You muft know," faid Wifeacre, " that, footfore
and weary with fearching for the cow from village to
village, from wildernefs to wildernefs, from enclofure
to enclofure, and from common to common, without
fuccefs, I was bending my fteps homeward, hot and
thirfty, when I efpied, at a fhort diftance, a refervoir
of water under the fhade of fome palm-trees. As I
approached it I faw feveral beautiful mares and
young foals fporting and grazing in a meadow on its
margin, and on a floping bank hard by a mare's
neft, in which were feveral eggs, fo large that even
the fmalleft could not be encompaffed by one's two
arms. As luck would have it, juft at that moment a
labourer, whofe hut was clofe by the refervoir, came
up ; fo, affuming ignorance, I inquired with apparent
indifference, what thofe large green oval-fhaped things
were, which were in the mare's-neft? 'Can it be
poffible,' faid he, 'that any one in this part of the
world, where we breed the beft horfes, does not know
a mare's egg when he fees it? Thofe are mares'
eggs, and the foals you fee yonder are of the fame
breed, and were only hatched yefterday. This is juft

the cheapeſt and beſt ſeaſon to buy them, and if you want any, now's the time. I do not own them; I wiſh I did; but I know the man that does, and juſt now he is in want of money to make up his rent, ſo that I think I could obtain you even the largeſt of them for five pagodas.' I told the man I was not going home at once, but ſhould probably take an opportunity to viſit the ſpot again before I did, when I would avail myſelf of his offer; for ſuch beautiful brood-mares as thoſe which had laid the eggs would be ſure to induce ſuch a judge of horſefleſh as I was to come again. Now, ſir, this is indeed a fine opportunity to get a thorough-bred horſe, which, in my opinion, ſhould not be loſt. Beſides, it ſeems to me, that it is wiſer and better to buy a horſe in the egg than after it has been hatched; for, with horſes as with men, all depends upon the training, and if we hatch it ourſelves, and train it ourſelves, it will be both docile and tractable; whereas, if we buy a horſe ready hatched, it may turn out a kicker, or a roarer, or a vicious brute, which the owner may only be too glad to get rid of. Then, too, it is difficult to know a horſe-chanter from a gentleman, the make up is ſo very perfect now-a-days, and even the moſt knowing are daily taken in."

The Gooroo and his diſciples were not long in making up their minds as to the purchaſe; indeed, they ſcarcely gave themſelves time for thought, but one and all declared that no time ſhould be loſt, and

as two heads are much better than one, that Noodle
fhould be joined to Wifeacre in the commiffion to
choofe and purchafe the egg. So the five pagodas
were placed in their hands, and they departed on
their errand at once.

When the Gooroo and Doodle, Zany and Foozle,
were left to themfelves, they began, each in his own
way, to fancy what kind of a horfe was to come out
of the egg. "Bleffed be the memory of him who
invented fleep," faid a wife man. No lefs bleffed
fhould be the memory of him who invented day-
dreams. Doodle's imagination had greater fcope
than that of the other three, from his habit of always
looking into the clouds with clofed eyes when deep in
contemplation. He had already fettled in his mind's
eye the fhape, fize, colour, and bearing of the fteed to
his perfect satisfaction, when fuddenly the thought
ftruck him that he was fomewhat in the dilemma of
the old lady who fold her chickens before the eggs
were hatched; for though the egg fhould come home
all right, how was it to be incubated? Full of this
thought, he turned to the Gooroo, faying, "Granted,
fir, that Noodle and Wifeacre felect the egg of a
thorough-bred mare, how are we to get at the foal
without fitting upon it to hatch it? and who, I
fhould like to know, is to do that, feeing that it
cannot be encompaffed by one's two arms? fo that
if you were to have ten hens for the purpofe, even
if you could manage to keep them on it, they

would not suffice. So what is to be done I don't know."

This speech of Doodle's took them quite by surprise, and it was some time before they got over it; so there they sat staring at each other, holding their tongues and never saying a word, till at length the Gooroo, unable to see his way out of the difficulty, which had come like a blight upon them, arose and retired into privacy, to think inwardly, as was his wont when matters of serious import required much thought and deliberation. At length, after he had been absent for more than three hours, he returned to the room where Doodle, Foozle, and Zany were, and said: " I have devoted much and serious confideration to folve the difficulty which Doodle has raifed, and it appears to me that there is no alternative but that one of us fhould fit upon the mare's egg for the purpofe of hatching it."

Upon hearing this the three difciples began each to make excufe. Zany faid, " It is quite impoffible that I can undertake to hatch the egg. See what I have to do. Firft, I have to go down to the river and fetch all the water that is wanted for daily ufe, as well for the purification of the mattam, as for ablution, and for cooking; then I have to go to the jungle to make faggots of fire-wood out of dried canes, and fo fully does this occupy my time, that often I can fcarcely find leifure to eat my dinner. No, no; I must not be afked to fit on the egg."

"Nor I either," put in Foozle. "Have I not to cater for you all? There is the food to buy and to cook. Night and day no reft, no ceffation from toil. Now rice to boil, and that requires no fmall care, if the nutritious *congèe*, the gluten and ftrength of the grain, is to be preferved; then curries to make, and pillaus to ftew; water all day long to be kept boiling, and cakes to prepare and bake for everybody, and all the world befides, when vifitors come to the mattam, fo that I fcarcely ever leave the kitchen, but pafs my days killing myfelf by inches, at the hot ftoves, whilft others take their fiefta at the third watch of the day, or enjoy the cool breeze in the firft watch of the night. No, no; I cannot be called upon to hatch the egg."

"As to hatching the egg," faid Doodle, "how is it poffible that I can find time to do it? Look at my daily duties. Firft, even before daybreak, I have to go down to the river and cleanfe my teeth, rinfe my mouth, wafh my face, purify my hands and feet, fhave away all hairs proferibed by our holy laws, ornament my brow with fandal-pafte, and obferve every ceremony to qualify me hereafter to fill the facred office of a gooroo; and then no fooner have I completed my toilet than I muft off to the garden to cull the choiceft opening buds of the flowers, bring them to the mattam with all reverence, weave them into long garlands, and fufpend them about our houfehold gods. Added to this I have to affift at the Poojei, the facrifices and offerings, which you, fir, make frequently in

the courfe of each day, after anointing and decorating
our deities. Such then being my office I have no
time to devote to hatching mares' eggs. No, no; I
cannot be made the incubator of the mare's egg."

To all thefe excufes, fo plaufibly urged, what could
the Gooroo object? The water muft be fetched and
the firewood provided; Zany could not be fpared.
Foozle was too good a cook to be taken away from
the kitchen; and Doodle's folemnity of manner was
neceffary to uphold the fanctity of the mattam. His
very ftep indicated the man of deep thought, and the
flow utterance and monotony of his words, the wifdom
of his fpeech. For feveral minutes the laft words of
Doodle were fucceeded by a profound filence. At
length the Gooroo faid : " Of a truth what you all
fay is very juft. Then, too, Noodle cannot find time
to hatch the egg; he has already more bufinefs on
his hands than he ever gets through. What with
receiving ftrangers and vifitors, who are pouring into
the mattam all day long, fome for one purpofe, fome
for another—now to feek advice, then to get difputes
arranged and fettled—he would only addle the egg,
even if he were difpofed to undertake the hatching it.
As for Wifeacre, the whole bufinefs of the mattam
would be at a ftandftill without his active and ready
aid. Whatever has to be done out of the village he
does; he goes to diftant merchants and buys clothing
for our bodies, and turns into money what we have to
fell; attends the markets and fairs, and even now, but

for his care and forethought, we fhould not have heard
of the mare's egg, which he and Noodle are gone to
buy. He can always find a mare's neft where another
would pafs it by; and from their great fimilarity to
afh-coloured pumpkins, even I might have miftaken
these mares' eggs for fome of thofe gourds. No, no;
Wifeacre muft not be fet to hatch the egg!

"Now it is quite clear that all of you, my children,
have ample work upon your hands, whilft I alone have
little or nothing to do but to fit ftill the livelong day.
I will therefore undertake to fupply a mother's place
to the egg, by placing it in my lap, and embracing it
with both arms, covering up its more expofed furface
with the fkirt of my robe and guarding it with tender-
nefs, hugging it to my bofom and nourifhing it with
the warmth of my life's breath. But we all know
that the duties of a nurfe require great care as to diet,
that nourifhment is neceffary to produce heat, and that
heat is the one great means of hatching eggs. Do
thou, therefore, my fon Foozle, lay in a good ftock of
fpices, of peppers and ginger, of cinnamon and cloves,
of garlic, and of that fpicieft of all fpices, which our
merchants bring from Perfia, pure affafœtida, which
will do more than all the others to increafe the natural heat of the body, and the circulation of its fluids.
I will eat nothing but fuch things as will aid me to
add warmth to my limbs, and in doing this I will
ftrive to make light of all my extra pains and trouble,
becaufe of the profpect of fpeedily producing a foal

from out of its fhell, and enjoy the delight of its gambols by anticipation, as a mother does thofe of her
child, as the firft reward of my prefent endurance."

Whilft the fubject of the egg's incubation was thus
under difcuffion within the walls of the mattam,
Noodle and Wifeacre, who had ftarted on their
miffion in the third watch, juft as the moon rofe,
with a walk of fome twenty-five miles before them—
for the mare's neft which Wifeacre had feen was juft
two kadams and a half from that dwelling—had
arrived at the margin of the refervoir, on the em-
bankment of which were clufters of afh-coloured
pumpkins, as fome people might have thought, but
which Wifeacre had already fatisfied his companion
were eggs in a mare's neft. Both were delighted to
find that no one had been before them to fecure the
prize, and, juft as luck would have it, there was
the identical labourer clofe to the eggs, as he had
been the day before, when Wifeacre had made the
difcovery. Greetings paffed between them, and the
labourer, who had fomething the matter with the fide
of his nofe, which made it neceffary for him to con-
tinually rub the cartilage with his fore-finger, and
which action had a curious effect upon his right eye,
as the lid kept rifing and falling every time he did fo,
called out to another man, at a fhort diftance, that
"the two young gentlemen had come to buy a mare's
egg," adding, that he hoped he would ufe them well,
as he had recommended them. To this Noodle

eagerly added, "Master, we have come a great way, knowing what a famous brood of horses you have, and we earnestly entreat you to give us one of these eggs, that we may get a horse out of it for the great and wise Gooroo Simple, whose disciples we are."

"How now, young gentlemen!" said the man, mistaking Noodle and Wiseacre, whose appearance was certainly somewhat verdant, for a couple of sappies; "what money have you got, for such a mare's nest as this is not to be met with every day, and eggs like these cost more than a few weeks' pocket-money. You must go to a cheaper market for a pony. My eggs are all thoroughbred ones, and I cannot part with them for less than a good round sum."

"Come, come," said Noodle, "let's have no chaffing, my man; this is not the first mare's nest we have seen, and we know very well that five pagodas will buy the best egg in the lot; so take your money, and let us have a ripe good one, instead of wasting our time any longer in idle talk."

"No offence, I hope, gentlemen," replied the man. "True, five pagodas is money; but who ever expects to get a thoroughbred horse for five pagodas? But as you seem such nice gentlemen, and I really have a desire to oblige you, upon one condition I will let you select one of these eggs at the price; but you must promise me not to breathe a word of my having done so to any living soul, because I have no intention of fupplying other folks with horfes at fuch a tremendous facrifice."

It was fome time before Wifeacre and Noodle could both agree upon which of the gourds their choice fhould fall. At length, however, they efpied one which, by lying on the hot, damp ground, had attained a brownifh, afh-coloured tint on the part not expofed to the fun, and hoping thus to fecure a valuable bay mare, they handed the five pagodas to the man, who immediately removed the one felected, which happened to be the largeft of the lot, and placed it on the ground by the fide of Wifeacre and Noodle. As it was now already in the fourth watch of the night, and no longer moonlight, they deter-mined to delay their return to the mattam till the morning.

They were fo elated with the fuccefsful iffue of their miffion, that neither could fleep, fo that even before daybreak they were up and ftirring, and, with the firft blufh of morning, ftarted on their way. Wifeacre carried the egg upon his head, and as his doing fo prevented him from looking ftraight before him, and their route lay acrofs many fields and rice plantations, Noodle walked in front of him to guide his way; and as they thus journeyed, they beguiled the time with pleafant talk. Full of the fubject then uppermoft in his thoughts, Wifeacre began the converfation by faying, "Of a truth there is wifdom in what was faid of old, that 'they who perform penance are forwarding their own affairs,' and we have now a proof of it before our eyes. There is our dear mafter, the good Gooroo, always doing penance for his own fins and thofe of others, and fee how his affairs profper, even when they feem to be all going the other way. He loft the cow, and here, for five pagodas, have we fecured for him a thoroughbred bay mare, which, at the very leaft, cannot be worth lefs than one hundred and fifty. Let the cow go; at beft fhe was an old one; and what is a cow compared to a horfe?"

"Nobody can doubt what you fay," replied Noodle. " 'Virtue brings its own reward,' and, 'pious actions alone afford delight; all elfe is but vanity.' From virtue not only pleafure but profit proceeds, and without virtue there is nothing but mifery and difgrace. Did not my honoured father for a long time practife many virtues, and did he not meet his reward in the end, and derive profit and delight in having me born to him? So, too, our blefled mafter; is he not noted for his virtue and piety throughout the land? and, as his reward, have we not been led hither to fecure for him the great wifh of his heart, a thoroughbred horfe, of great value, at lefs than the coft of a dog?"

"Can this be doubted?" faid Wifeacre. "From good actions good will arife; from evil actions, evil. 'If you fow a caftor-oil tree, can you hope to produce ebony?' As we fow, we muft expect to reap; wifdom produces wifdom; folly, folly."

Thus counting their gains before the egg was hatched, and ſtringing together many of the pearls of wiſdom which had fallen, from time to time, from the lips of the Gooroo, Noodle and Wiſeacre beguiled the way, till about the ſecond watch of the morning, when they reached a wood through which they had to paſs. Full of the bright viſion of the beautiful bay mare his fancy had conjured up, Wiſeacre forgot for the moment the ripe gourd which he carried on his head, and, in paſſing under the low branches of a tree, it was daſhed out of his hands, which were merely held up to keep it in its poſition, and fell with ſuch force upon the ground as to be daſhed into pieces, whilſt he, in attempting to ſtay its fall, over-balanced himſelf, and fell into the middle of a thorn buſh, lacerating his fleſh and tearing his clothes, and ſtarting, at the ſame time, a hare, which had been ſitting on her haunches cloſe by the ſpot where the gourd had tumbled to pieces.

All this had occurred ſo ſuddenly that Noodle, who was a few ſteps in advance, could render no aſſiſtance till the miſchief had been fairly done; but ſeeing the hare ſtart out of the buſhes he called out to Wiſeacre, juſt as the latter had picked himſelf up, " I ſay, I ſay ; look there, look there ! There goes the foal out of the egg, and there's not a moment to be loſt, or it will get away ;" ſaying which, off he ſcampered, followed by Wiſeacre, through the buſhes and under-wood, the murderous thorns tearing the clothes and

flesh of both, whilst the hare, upon the approach of her
purfuers, bounded forward over hill and dale, acrofs
fields, through woods, and only refting every now and
then, as if, in the enjoyment of the fun, she did it to
lure them on.

Perfpiring at every pore, with beating hearts, deaf
from excitement, and faint from the lofs of blood ;
puffing and blowing, regularly done up, and with
uneafy rumbling ftomachs, they at length flung
themfelves at full length upon the ground, worn out
and haraffed with fatigue, and dead beat ; whilft the
hare, finding the fun done, looked back quietly once
or twice, and then betaking herfelf to cover, was loft
to view. Shortly after, regardlefs of their great
fatigue, Noodle and Wifeacre rofe up again to renew
the fearch ; but their only reward was frefh wounds
from the relentlefs thorns, as they went limping in
every direction over ftones and ftumps, for the wicked
pufs had left them in the lurch, and the young foal
was nowhere to be feen. The fun had already fet, and
it was not till the firft watch of the night that, footfore
and bleeding from numberlefs wounds, and weak and
famifhed, having tafted no food for the whole day,
they at length reached the mattam.

Once more fafe within its gates they gave way to
loud lamentations, cafting themfelves on the ground,
fmiting their breafts and mouths, tearing the hair off
their heads, and manifefting in every way the depths
of their mifery and defpair. " Hem ! Hem ! Woe is

is me! Woe is me!" cried Wiseacre. "Oh, that I never was born!" put in Noodle. "Evils come by twelve fingers'-length, and only go away by the breadth of one! What will become of us! Was ever misery like ours! Who can help us! Who can save us!"

Their noisy lamentations soon brought the Gooroo and their fellow disciples, Doodle and Foozle and Zany, to their aid; but it was some time before they could render them any assistance; for they looked at their swollen limbs and features, at their tattered clothes, and bleeding feet and hands, without being able to unriddle the mystery, and in perfect bewilderment they all stood by as if bereft of their senses. At length Foozle and Zany raised up Wiseacre, and the Gooroo and Doodle helped to place Noodle upon his feet. They pressed the sufferers to their bosoms, dried up their tears, and staunched their wounds, bidding them to be comforted now, to calm their grief, and to tell them what had happened. Upon this Wiseacre took courage, and, with Noodle's aid, narrated in detail every circumstance that had befallen them since they had left the mattam on the previous day, not even omitting the conversation which preceded their great disaster. Warming with his subject as he drew near its close, he broke out with, "Hem, sir, had you but seen the beautiful foal which we have lost, you would not wonder at the depth of our grief. Never in my whole life have I beheld so beautiful a creature! Swift as the wind, of an ash colour mixed

F

with black, clean limbed, and graceful in all its movements! In form and size it somewhat resembled a hare, and as it sprang out of its shell, it was full a cubit in length. And then, only a foal just burst into life, it pricked up its two ears so daintily, and cocking up its tail, which was two fingers' breadth in length, it extended and stretched out its four beautiful little legs to the ground, and dashed off at full speed with such swiftness and impetuosity, that no words can do justice to its paces, nor can any one conceive their velocity but those who have witnessed them. So rapid were they that the beautiful creature seemed to fly instead of to run, and indeed I do not hesitate to say that such another foal has never been seen in the world."

When Wiseacre had finished speaking, Zany, Doodle, and Foozle, joined him and Noodle in bewailing the loss of such a paragon of a steed; but the Gooroo, assuming an air of indifference, as the fox did when he declared the grapes to be sour, said, " Do not grieve thus, my children. It is true my five pagodas are gone; but after what Wiseacre has told us of the foal, it is quite as well that that is gone too. If as a little foal it could run in that manner, who would be able to keep his seat upon its back when full grown? I am now old, and such a steed would not suit me. Indeed, if any one were to offer me one like it for nothing, I would not accept it. So let us say no more about it; but do you, Noodle and Wiseacre, have your wounds dressed, and take that repose and nourish-

ment of which you ſtand ſo much in need. So giving
them his bleſſing, the Gooroo diſmiſſed his diſciples
for the night.

STORY THE THIRD.

THE GOOROO'S RIDE ON OX-BACK.

A fcorching fun and no fhade; the Ox ferves for a canopy, and his driver demands payment for its ufe; the Padeiyachi appointed judge; legal niceties of leave and licenfe; ftory of a favoury relifh for cold boiled rice, and payment for the treat; judgment of the Padeiyachi: the fhadow of Money for the fhadow of the Ox.

ITY it was that the egg from the mare's neft did not furnifh the good Gooroo with the bay mare which Wifeacre had already beftridden fo many times in imagination on the eventful morning of its purchafe; for, not long after that unfortunate adventure, a neceffity arofe for making a long and tedious journey, when fhe would have been of the greateft fervice to him and his dif-

ciples. As it was, feeing that without fome beaft of
burden upon which the Gooroo and his five followers
might ride by turns, the journey could not be accom-
plifhed, it was deemed prudent to hire a fteady old ox,
whofe horns had been feared to prevent their growth
when he was yet but a calf, for the hire of which they
agreed to give three fanams a day ; and having devoted
the firft watch of the morning to the home duties of
the mattam, they fet out juft as the fun was fhining
forth in full radiance as he rofe towards the meridian.

For the firft hour the way was a little fheltered from
the heat, which was neverthelefs very great, as it was
juft at the hotteft feafon of the year, and the fummer
was more than ufually oppreffive ; but after that they
entered upon a wide and boundlefs fandy plain, without a fingle tree or bufh, or any other fhelter from the
scorching rays of the fun, which fell perpendicularly
upon them. The venerable Gooroo, but little accuf-
tomed to mifs the cool fhade of the mattam, foon
fuccumbed to the heat, and bending like an ear of
ripening corn as they flowly jogged along, or rather
refembling the death-like *paffoun-kirey* with its dried-
up, drooping, and withered ftalk, would have fallen off
the back of the ox, had not his difciples perceived his
woeful plight and lifted him gently to the ground.
As it was, when they placed him carefully on
the fandy plain, he was fo overcome that he lay
ftretched out without power to move, more like one
dead than a living being. In this ftrait they were

at a lofs what to do, for they all feared he would die by the way; as, though they fanned him with their clothes, the heat of the fun's rays, and the burning fand upon which they fell, made all their efforts of no avail.

Zany, who was ftanding by the ox, perceived that under the animal's body, as he ftood on his four legs, there were a few inches of fhade; fo he went up to Noodle and Doodle, who were deep in confultation of what was beft to be done, and told them of the difcovery he had made. Wifeacre and Foozle, hearing this, led the ox carefully up to the fpot upon which the poor old Gooroo lay ftretched, and whilft Zany held the animal's head, Noodle and Doodle each took hold of one of the fore legs of the old beaft, and Wifeacre and Foozle each of one of its hind legs, fixing its tail in pofition by preffing againft it with their heads, and in this manner they proceeded to guide it till it fairly ftood over the proftrate Gooroo, and ferved as a canopy to fhield him from the fun's fcorching rays. Having placed their beloved mafter thus in comparative comfort, they redoubled their efforts to cool the air by fanning him with their clothes, in which they were greatly aided by a cool breeze which fprang up. Gradually the Gooroo revived and, feeling refrefhed, remounted the ox, when the party proceeded on their journey, and juft as the fhades of evening were falling, reached a little village, where they halted for the night.

Now, it will be remembered, that the ox-driver had

taken no part in placing his animal over the proſtrate
body of the Gooroo. Indeed, he had purpoſely left
the ſpot the moment that Wiſeacre had taken hold of
the halter by which he had led it; for out of that act
of ownerſhip exerciſed by a ſervant of the Gooroo he
intended to make an extra profit, as we ſhall now ſee.
Accordingly, when our travellers had taken poſſeſſion
of their quarters in the village choultry, which by day

ſerved for a temple and a court of juſtice, but by night
offered its ſhelter to the wayfarer, Noodle, who, as
ſenior diſciple, carried the money bag, tendered the
three fanams, as agreed, to the ox-driver for the day's
hire.

"What is this for?" said the driver; "that is by no means enough."

"Not enough?" asked Noodle; "why, is it not the full sum agreed upon? What more would you have?"

"What more would I have," put in the man; "what more would I have? Why, what's my due, and no mistake. Quite true, I was to have three fanams for the use of my ox as a beast of burden, and for that I will take them in full satisfaction for the day's ride. I scorn to impose upon any man, and I am not going to let any man impose on me. What's right, is right. Without saying by your leave, or making any bones about the matter, did not Master Wiseacre take the ox away from where he stood, and turn him into a canopy against the scorching rays of the sun? And did you not all five assist and place him over the old Gooroo, who would have perished miserably but for the shadow of my ox? Now what belonged to my ox belonged to me, so that his shadow was my property, of the enjoyment of which that act of yours deprived me. Am I not to be reimbursed for the loss I thus sustained? I must be paid for that too; and as without it the poor old gentleman would have died, I am not going to be put off with a trifle."

Whilst the driver was thus disputing his fare, Wiseacre and Foozle, Doodle and Zany had come out of the choultry to see what the row was about, and no sooner had the man set up his claim for compensation for the loss of the shadow of the ox, which they had

wrongfully converted to their own ufe, than they one
and all began to cry out fhame, and charge him with
attempting to impofe upon them. But he was not to
be put down, and ftood upon his rights; for no one
could fay that there was not a fhadow for him to found
a claim upon, and he knew enough of law to be fatisfied with even that for its foundation. The difpute at
length became fo loud and furious that gradually the
villagers came flocking to the fpot; firft the women,
as was natural, to fatisfy their curiofity: then the
men, as was no lefs natural, to fee what the women
were about, till at length a noify mob ftood around
the choultry, fome fiding with the difciples of the
Gooroo, and fome with the ox-driver; but all voci-
ferating and fhouting, and thofe, who knew leaft of the
merits of the cafe, the loudeft and moft boifterous of
the partifans of the fide they had feverally efpoufed.

When the row was at its height, the chief of the
village came forth to quell it. He was a Padeiyachi,
and though only a fuperior kind of farm labourer, a
man of ready wit, who knew how to make his authority refpected. By way of appeafing the fray, he at
once adjourned the meeting into the Court of the
choultry, and having feated himfelf upon the bench
from whence he daily difpenfed juftice, he afked the
litigants whether they would be content to place
the matter in difpute in his hands, and abide by his
decifion. This having been agreed to, the ox-driver
ftated his cafe, cleverly importing into it many circum-

ftances which, though quite irrelevant to the matter in difpute, he thought might throw duft in the eyes of the judge; and which led Noodle and Doodle, Wife-acre, Foozle and Zany, ever and anon to interrupt him, and brought down upon them a " Silence in the Court!" from the dignitary who occupied the judgment feat.

Having heard both fides, Noodle, on the part of the Gooroo, having argued that the ox-driver had given leave and licenfe, had ftood by, allowed, and permitted the ox to be ufed for the purpofe, and therefore had no ftanding in Court, the Padeiyachi thus proceeded to addrefs them:

" I myfelf, fome years ago, when returning home from a diftant journey, came in the evening to a very large choultry, or rather a caravanfara; for, befides lodging, they fupplied for money to thofe that came to it every thing they might require in the way of refrefhment. Now, it fo happened that I had fcarcely money enough with me to defray my travelling ex-penfes; fo when they afked me if I required any-thing, I replied in the negative; for though it is bad enough to be poor, it is always a great deal worfe to appear fo. At the end of the room, over a brifk fire, was a pot of cabobs, and clofe by a fpit, reft-ing upon two fupports, was laden with a large and delicious leg of mutton, which, as the fat browned and frizzled, fent forth a moft tantalizing odour to the fenfitive perceptions of a hungry man. Now, I had

not omitted to bring with me a cloth full of boiled
rice, as is cuſtomary when one goes on a journey;
but of lime-juice or pepper-water I had none; for I
had been obliged to huſband my means in order that
they might laſt out till I ſhould reach home, and ſo to
content myſelf with the bareſt neceſſaries, luxuries being

quite out of the queſtion. The favory ſmell of the mutton made me feel quite a gnawing at my ſtomach, and
though I would fain have kept the cold boiled rice for
my breakfaſt, I could not withſtand the craving appe-

tite it produced, and so asking permission to sit by the
fire and turn the spit for a while, I took out my bundle of rice, and whilst I gratified the cravings of nature by eating the rice, I no less enjoyed the savoury
odour which proceeded from the cabobs and the mutton, as I consumed my frugal supper.

" I had a long day's travel before me, so I got up
betimes, intending to depart with the first watch of the
morning.   Judge of my astonishment when I reached
the door to find the master of the caravansara there,
who refused to allow me to depart till I had paid for
the savoury odour of the mutton, with which I had
tickled my palate by the agency of my nose.

" At first I thought the man was chaffing me on
account of my poverty; but soon found that he was
in earnest; so, growing very angry, I asked him if he
took me for a fool, and one that he could so easily
impose upon, as to demand payment for having merely
sniffed the savoury odour of a dish he was cooking.
In short, we both got warm, and to put an end to the
quarrel, agreed to go before the chief man of the
village.

" He was fortunately a man who could not be
bought over by bribes, was courteous to all, and never
forgot that he who dispenses the laws must be a gentleman both by habit and thought, must weigh well
both sides of the matter submitted to him, and only
give judgment after mature deliberation.   Then, too,
he was well read in the Darma Shastra, that great and

glorious monument of our laws, which are the perfec-
tion of human intellect. He was indeed a great and
learned Shaftri, a lawyer fuch as one can feldom hope
to meet with.

"Now, liften to his judgment, which he did not
deliver till he had confulted a great many books,
all of which lay open before him, as he fpoke in the
following terms :—

" ' It is for him who ate of the mutton to pay for
the mutton in money; but for him who fniffed of
the odour of the mutton to pay for it by the fniff of
money. That is my judgment.'

" Whereupon, calling the mafter of the caravanfara
to him, he placed a bag of copper fanams on the table
before him, and ftretching his hand acrofs the back of
the head of my obdurate creditor, he paid him in his
own coin, by rubbing and fcrubbing his nofe for
feveral minutes amongft the contents of the bag, faying all the while, ' Now, my good friend, pay yourfelf
liberally, there is no ftint; fniff away and enjoy
the rich odour to your heart's content.' Then, when
the mafter of the caravanfara at length found breath
to fay, ' Enough, enough ! I am quite fatisfied ; my
poor nofe ! my poor nofe ! it is coming off; ftay, I
pray you !' down went the head again and again,
each time it was raifed up, till, overcome by the
exertion, the learned Shaftri at length defired the fatisfaction of the debt to be placed on the records of the
Court.

"You have heard this. Was it not juftice? Was it not law? This decifion of the wife Shaftri is the precedent upon which I have founded the judgment of the Court in the cafe now before it. For the journeying hither upon the ox the three fanams, already paid, are payment in full; for the ufe of the fhadow of the ox, the fhadow of money muft fuffice. But as the fun has already gone down, and in fuch cafes fpeedy execution fhould follow as a matter of courfe, the Court in its difcretion will fubftitute the chink of money for its fhadow." So, taking hold of a heavy bag of fanams, which, whilft delivering judgment he had placed before him, he held it up and made the contents chink; and, having fuddenly feized on the ox-driver, he repeatedly and fharply ftruck the money-bag againft his ear, fhouting out each time, "Doft hear? doft hear? Chink, chink; doft hear?"

"Oh my head! oh my ear! Enough, enough!" cried the ox-driver. "I am fully paid for the fhadow of my ox. Defift! pray defift!"

The claim raifed by the ox-driver having been thus fully fatisfied, the Gooroo faid: "I am a man of peace, and care not to be mixed up again in fuch unfeemly quarrels. I cannot endure this vexation. Take away thy ox, I have no more occafion for him; and as the remainder of the journey is fhort, in the morning I will proceed on foot, refting from time to time when fatigued." Saying which the good Gooroo turned to the Padeiyachi, and thanking him for the equitable way in which he had delivered judgment in a cafe fo furrounded with difficulties, he gave him his blefling and difmiffed him.

STORY THE FOURTH.

FISHING FOR A HORSE.

Wifeacre goes to a field, and performs his ablutions; the Temple of
Ayinar, and the votive fteed; Natural Philofophy and as natural
doubts; the horfe in the water, and how to catch it; Anglers never
at a lofs; fubftitutes for line and hook; the nibble and bite; a long
pull and a ftrong pull, and lofs of the line and hook; the promifed
fteed.

N the whole, the Gooroo
and his difciples were well
pleafed to have got rid
of the ox and his mafter,
and, dreading the
heat, while anxious
to continue their
journey, they were
ready, at early cock
crow, to begin the
day's march. Never-
thelefs, as the vener-
able man was un-
able to make a rapid
progrefs, they had to
travel at a flow pace, and had not yet completed the
firft kadam, when the heat became fo intenfe, that, to
efcape the fcorching rays of the fun, they were glad

to turn out of the road, and seek the shade of some trees, at a little distance from their direct route, which grew near a reservoir, intending, in this cool grove, to await the afternoon's breeze.

Here they reposed for some time in delicious silence, till after a while Wiseacre, having first sought the privacy of the fields, hastened to make his ablutions in the cool water. On the margin of the reservoir stood a temple dedicated to *Ayinar*, the son of Vishnoo, and close to it was placed the life-size figure of a horse of newly-baked clay, a votive offering of some pious soul for recovery from a severe and dangerous illness. The reservoir was full up to the brim with the most limpid and translucent water, lying calm and still in the noon-day heat, and upon its furface the ftatue was mirrored with ftartling clearnefs. Wifeacre gazed long and earneftly in filent aftonifhment at the phenomenon before him. He could not divine the caufe of the myftery. Water was not the natural element of a horfe ; how could it ftand there in apparent eafe and comfort, entirely fubmerged ? Abforbed in profound meditation (for Wifeacre was already famed at the mattam as moft learned and deep in the philofophy of caufe and effect), the thought fuddenly ftruck him that external objects are reflected by water, and that the object which he faw was, after all, but the fhadow or reprefentation of the terra - cotta horfe ftanding upon the bank of the refervoir. He compared the ftatue on land with the animal feen in the water; he faw that in colour and fize both were the fame. He examined each figure with careful judgment and painftaking difcrimination, until he arrived at a fatisfactory folution of the difficulty, and became firmly convinced that what he had firft taken for a live horfe was in reality nothing more than an image or fhadow caft upon the polifhed furface of the water by the intercepted rays of light. It was indeed a great difcovery, worthy of a pupil of the wife Gooroo Simple. As Wifeacre was contemplating the beft way of turning it to account by communicating it to other equally learned perfons, a gentle breeze arofe, fanning the water with its foft carefs into an anfwering fmile or ripple, and the wind increafing, the pool became much agitated, whilft at the fame moment the fuppofed fhadow horfe beftirred itfelf, and feemed reftlefs. Wifeacre remarked the change, but feeing that the ftatue remained immoveable, whilft the animal which he had believed to be its reflection con-

tinued to move, he changed his former opinion, and was perfuaded that he had deceived himfelf in his previous deductions. "If the horfe that one fees at the bottom of the refervoir," faid he to himfelf, "were only the reflection of that which is placed upon the edge of the pool, it would not ftir nor move as it does; for the reflection ought to be as ftationary

as the real object! It follows, then, of courſe, that
the reſtleſs animal in the water muſt be different from
that which ſtands paſſive and inmoveable on the
bank." Nevertheleſs, he wiſhed to be more certain
of the fact, haſty concluſions being too often erroneous;
ſo he picked up a large ſtone, and threw it with all
his might into the pool, at the exact ſpot where the
horſe was gently curvetting beneath its ſurface, uttering, at the ſame time, loud cries, and making energetic
paſſes with his hands, in order to frighten it, and
make it change its poſition. The ſtone, daſhed with
ſuch violence into the water, conſiderably increaſed
the action of the ripple, and the horſe below became
in conſequence fearfully excited. It ſtruggled, ſtamped,
leaped, kicked, reared, and plunged with ſuch fierce
impetuoſity, as only an angry animal could diſplay.
Seeing this, Wiſeacre no longer doubted for a moment
that the horſe at the bottom of the reſervoir was
actually a living one. Tranſported with joy, he ran
back to tell this good news to the Gooroo, and to
concert with Noodle and Doodle, Zany and Foozle,
the means by which they might render themſelves
maſters of ſuch a high-ſpirited creature. Amazed
and delighted, they all aroſe at once, and hurried off
to the ſpot, and ſeeing themſelves the furious efforts
of the horſe to regain the land, they entered at once
into deep conſultation upon the matter, firſt liſtening
with deference to Wiſeacre's minute detail of what
he had obſerved, and following with profound atten-

tion his line of argument, they arrived at a clear and unanimous conviction of the truth and cleverness of his reasoning. This was no hasty resolve; and in their consultation, the five circumstances so essential to a formal conference had all been duly confidered. *Firstly.* The tangible means demanded attention. *Secondly.* The fruits to be expected had to be brought under view in their four admitted aspects of good works, wealth, pleasure, and paradise, wealth being again subdivided into riches, money, or goods and chattels. *Thirdly.* The choice of time and opportunity for commencing the work called forth many remarks; and *Fourthly.* Every objection which could be urged against it had to be satisfactorily answered. All these points settled, there still remained, *fifthly,* to determine whether the matter under consideration was worth the trouble, and whether it ought to be done. The Gooroo and his followers never entered lightly upon any undertaking; and as they discussed these weighty points with their customary ability and perspicuity, the good man was touched by the affectionate anxiety they evinced for his comfort and relief from the fatigues of travel. Difcussion ended, action must follow. The questions to be decided were the means of capture, and the manner of doing it. But they could not agree. Zany advised that one of them should jump into the pool, bind the horse with cords, and compel it to come out by the rest dragging it ashore. This plan, though the most sure and prompt, was too perilous, as no one poffeffed fufficient courage to attempt to put it into practice. Foozle thought the horfe might be decoyed or coaxed by a fieve of corn fhaken in its fight, but there was this infur-mountable objection, that they had neither corn nor fieve to fhake. Nothing daunted, Wifeacre, whofe turn it was now to fpeak, drew forth a fickle from their ftores, and propofed that they fhould ufe it as a fifh-hook, tie a line to it, and bait it with the boiled rice they, like other travellers, carried with them to eat on the way. Doodle and Noodle coincided, and general approval having been given to this propofi-tion, they ftraightway fet to work to put it into practice. Like all clever anglers, their refources were inex-hauftible. For a line they ufed part of the Gooroo's turban, and triumphantly forced the fickle into the mafs of rice; but by fome fatality it came out again with not a grain upon it. Rich in contrivance, Doodle tore off part of an ancient garment that he wore about his perfon, and directing Wifeacre to tie the rice up in it, he buried the fickle's point deep within the bundle. Loud applaufe rewarded this fuccefsful feat. All being ready, they approached the pool, and caft the line as anglers do, into the water, which, as it received the bait, became more difturbed than ever, and the horfe began to leap, to kick, and plunge in fuch a wild and frantic manner that the anxious group upon the bank, feized with alarm and overpowering terror left he fhould rufh out upon them,

let go their hold of the line, and fled for the bare life
of them.

Wiseacre alone retained his presence of mind.
He continued at his post, and firmly holding the
untwisted turban, to the end of which the sickle was
attached, as the ripple subsided, softly drew nearer

to the pool, and seeing the horse less excited, to keep
him quiet "So-ho'd" him, using all the many
gentle and endearing epithets with which it is the way
of the world to cajole and gammon a rustic horse into
subjection, trolling the bundle of rice all the while in
the most appetising way under the poor creature's very
nose.

Presently he felt a nibble, then a tug at his line,

but not feeing the dark heads of fome large fifh, which were fnapping at the cloth to get at the rice, he fhouted, "Help! help! the horfe has fwallowed the bait! Come back! come back! there's nothing to fear!"

Peeping from behind the trees, Doodle and Noodle, Foozle and Zany, perceived the figns made by Wife-acre, and hearing his fhouts of triumph, they took courage and emerged from their hiding-place. Warily approaching, and ftepping daintily, once more they laid hold of the line, hauling it carefully in, when fuddenly, the cloth and rice being gone, a ftrong re-fiftance enfued, arifing, as they one and all declared, from the horfe having gorged the bait. "Bravo!" they cried, laughing loudly, "the horfe is our own! Pull away! pull away! A long pull, a ftrong pull, and a pull altogether;" and, uniting the whole of their ftrength, they grafped the poor old turban, which, having feen much fervice, gave way like burnt thread, and down toppled all five on their backs, with their heels aloft in the air, while the fickle, now fixed in a ftout branch that had fallen from a tree above, repofed with the turban and the horfe at peace in the water.

A traveller who was paffing by, and had watched their proceedings for fome time in filence, without comprehending in the leaft what they were about, after their fall approached and inquired what new game they were playing. His good-humoured face and honeſt greeting aſſured them of his ſympathy; ſo they poured into his ears the tale of their angling to catch the horſe, and how their line had unfortunately broken at the very moment they believed they had got poſſeſſion of him. The ſtranger, perceiving the kind of cuſtomers he had to deal with, yet wiſhing to undeceive them kindly, as one does thoſe whoſe acts, although not of the wiſeſt, ſtill proceed from good motives, ſaid, "Do you not ſee that the horſe in the

water is but the ſhadow of the ſtatue on the bank? If you ſtill doubt it, I will convince you in ſpite of yourſelves."

So taking the cloth from his ſhoulders, he threw it like a veil over the terra-cotta horſe, and immediately the horſe was inviſible in the pool. The diſciples of the Gooroo, now fully convinced of their miſtake, ſought to make excuſes for the falſe ſtep into which they had been betrayed, by acquainting the traveller with their anxiety to procure a horse at a small coft, on which their beloved but worn-out mafter could ride. They then told him all the particulars of their difaftrous adventures, not only as fifliers, but as finders of mares' nefts, and the cruel impofition of the previous day, by which the Gooroo had nearly loft his life, fuffocated by the heat, and the troubles confequent upon the roguifli conduct of the ox-driver.

The ftranger foon gathered from this recital of their misfortunes that thefe poor fellows were of a clafs fo common in the world, more fools than knaves, that it would be a hopelefs tafk to enlighten their ignorance; but pitying their condition, he faid kindly, "I have an old lame horfe which may be ferviceable to you for the journeys you make. Fanam or kafhoo I do not require, but prefent it to you as a gift. Follow me to the neighbouring village, and reft beneath my roof this night."

So faying, he took them away with him, their whole party congratulating each other upon having met with fuch a noble and generous protector, no lefs than upon the profpect of at length poffeffing a horfe.

And fo it is written: "A prudent man trufts to a true friend in the day of trouble, for no one overcomes adverfity without a friend." No; not upon mother or wife, brother, or even upon one's own fon, can a man fo firmly repofe as upon the bofom of a tried friend. When all others fail him, let him place his truft in him, and he will ride fecurely through a fea of trouble.

STORY THE FIFTH.

THE GOOROO ON HORSEBACK.

Riches and pleasure; Don't look a gift-horse in the mouth; the equestrian order; lucky days; the procession; the tax of pride; toll to pay; story of an unsavoury tax and sweet-money; the horse in the pound; the pocket teaches humility; the Valloovan turned veterinarian; a Rarey-show.

HE Goo-
roo Sim-
ple and
his five at-
tendants,
Noodle,
and Doo-
dle, Wife-
acre, Za-
ny, and
Foozle,
accom-
panied
the stran-

ger to his house, and having bid them welcome, their host asked them to rest themselves after their fatigues until the hour of supper arrived. He was far from being a rich man; for to constitute wealth there must be eight gifts:—money, the principal of all; corn or land, crops or rents; children—for what are riches without heirs? and the lute is only sweet music to them that know not the sound of their children's prattle; chattels and personal property; relations; friends; and slaves to do one's bidding. Without these how can a man obtain the eight pleasures of life: good living, fine clothing, delicious perfumes, flowers and fruits; betel and areka; a beloved wife, gifted musicians, and a bed of roses—a couch of flowers to rest upon? As their new friend did not possess all these blessings, he could not be called rich; indeed, he was a poor man; but then he was benevolent and right-minded, and loved to exercise the holy rite of hospitality to strangers, treating them with disinterested generosity; so when the evening repast was served he regaled them with ghee, and tyer milk and rice, betel leaves and nuts, together with tobacco, and whatever else was requisite, in abundance.

The next morning he sent for the horse, which was out at grass, either on the common or by the road side, as the case might be, and stepping it out before the Gooroo, prayed him to accept it as a free gift, and a mark of his great friendship and consideration. The horse was twenty years old, it was true; blind of one eye, and shorn of one ear; lame in his fore leg, and with one of his hind legs a little short and contracted;

neverthelefs he could "go," and was for that reafon
a moft valuable gift to their venerable mafter; fo the
Gooroo and his difciples were overjoyed thus to obtain
poffeffion of the object of their ardent defires, and made
light of defects which were as nothing in their eyes
compared to the diftinction a horfe conferred upon
their miffion.   Gathering round it, they examined the
animal in filent admiration for a time, until Zany, to

whofe charge it was to be confided, began to pat its
head; Foozle to ftroke its back and other parts of its
body; Wifeacre, as a judge of horfeflefh, to lift up
firft one foot and then another, fcraping the hoof of
each; Doodle, with an eye to the general effect,

feparated the hairs of the tail, fmoothing them out
carefully, fo as to give it a flowing appearance; Noodle
fed it with grafs, which he plucked up by the roots,
that none of its nourifhment might be loft, wiping the
poor old beaft's eyes at the fame time, and rubbing the
fore place where the ear was not. After lavifhing
thefe tender cares upon the horfe, the next thing was
to have it faddled and bridled for the Gooroo to ride;
but how could they, in fuch an out-of-the-way place,
obtain harnefs fuitable to the dignity of their mafter?
Plunged into this frefh dilemma, their hoft again
came to their aid by finding fome of the old trappings.
But the faddle was torn, and was minus a crupper,
without which it would flip over the animal's ears on
the firft hill he fhould defcend; fo they cut fome
*pālic-kodi,** and plaiting the bines into a cord, made
a loop for his tail. Then the old rufty bit was without head-gear or bridle; but this they fupplied with
twifted hay-bands which were lying in the field.
Then, too, the ftirrups were without leathers, and
there was no belly-band to fix the whole. Wifeacre
in hafte ran off to a village hard by, from whence he
brought fome cart harnefs, and converting it into the
miffing articles, he fafhioned what was left into a mar-
tingale befitting the rank of his mafter.

When all this had been done, it was already the
evening of the tenth day of the moon's age, and the
next was Monday the eleventh, itfelf a day of ill-luck,

* Asclepias volubilis, a parafitical plant.

rendered thus more unlucky ftill; fo Wifeacre was
told to ftudy the true rules of aftrology, which he had
got from a learned Poorahita at the village feftival of
laft year, and thus make himfelf mafter of Fate; for
the Gooroo never commenced an important undertaking on an unlucky day, and thefe, every one knows,
are the 4th, the 6th, the 8th, the 9th, the 11th, the
12th, the 14th, and the 15th of the moon's age, unlefs
they are made otherwife by falling on the lucky days
of the week; and are thefe not thus fet forth by the
rules of aftrology?   "If the 8th day of the moon's age
falls on a Sunday, the 9th on a Monday, the 6th on
a Tuefday, the 3rd on a Wednefday, the 9th on a
Thurfday, the 13th on a Friday, and the 14th on a
Saturday, then thefe lucky days ferve to counteract
the ill-luck of the week in which they fall; but if the
12th day of the moon's age falls on a Sunday, the
11th on a Monday, the 5th on a Tuefday, the 2nd on
a Wednefday, the 6th on a Thurfday, the 8th on a
Friday, and the 9th on a Saturday, then not only are
thofe days themfelves unlucky, but they alfo influence
the luck of the week, even rendering the 2nd and
5th days of the moon's age unlucky, though the
2nd, the 5th, the 7th, the 10th, and the 13th are
otherwife its lucky days."

So the unlucky days were paffed over by the
Gooroo and his followers in taking their reft and in
making preparations for their journey; and when the
fortunate period arrived, the people of the village,

Ll

men, women, and children, crowded round the difciples of the Gooroo, as with much folemnity they raifed their mafter in their arms and placed him on the back of their brave old fteed, the fpectators the while cheering and clapping their hands, and making the air ring with their acclamations.

Foozle, as Groom of the Stole, walked on one fide, and adjufted the garments of the Gooroo; Wifeacre, now Mafter of the Horfe, gave his mafter the requifite inftructions by which he could hold on and keep his proper balance; Zany, in right of his new office of equerry, walked in front with the ftraw bridle in his hand, and pulled the horfe forward to keep him going; Doodle, the whipper-in, went behind and forced the animal to advance by pufhing him with the left hand, the right hand dealing out at the fame time enlivening blows with a heavy ftick; whilft Noodle, as chief minifter, walked on the other fide of the Gooroo, with raifed arms ready to uphold him if he fhould totter. The Gooroo himfelf held on bravely, grafping with one hand the pommel of the faddle, and the horfe's mane with the other.

Once fairly ftarted, Zany preceded the cortège, and fhouted with a loud voice, warning the people to get out of the way, and leave the road clear for the paffage of the great Gooroo Simple; calling upon them to do homage to fo illuftrious a perfonage, whofe praifes he proclaimed; and repeating from time to time, in a voice that was heard afar off: " Look out !

look out! take care! take care! clear the way!" led on the cavalcade in triumph.

At length they arrived at a toll-gate, and were paffing through as became their high eftate and dignity, when the gate-keeper ftopped them and demanded the toll for the horfe, which he faid was five fanams.

"What do you fay?" exclaimed Wifeacre, ftupified and thrown all of a heap, as it were, by the extravagant demand of the man; "You are chaffing us! Demand toll for a horfe ridden by a Gooroo!" "We are not Vaifyas and merchants," put in Doodle, "mere grovellers in the dirt; nor does the horfe carry a bale of goods, that we fhould be called upon to pay toll like a Chitty packman. Our horfe has been prefented as a gift by a generous friend, who, feeing that our venerable mafter could not walk without great trouble, had compaffion on his weaknefs, and gave him this fteed. By what authority do you claim toll? It is a grofs fraud, an act of cruel injuftice! Have you lefs pity than he who gave the horfe?"

But all his clever pleadings, arguments, and complaints were of no avail. The heart of the toll-gate keeper was not open to pity, and as he faw no fanams forthcoming, he pufhed Zany on one fide, and feized the bridle, faying, he "would not let the horfe go until they had rendered tribute to the ftate;" adding with an angry and refolute air, "Come, pay the toll; here is no exemption for volunteers: Gooroo or groom, Pariar or prieft, it's all the fame to me. The toll I demand, and the toll I will have, whether from Brahman, Vaifya, or Chitty!"

Doodle and Wifeacre ftill continued their entreaties and threats by turn, but at laft were obliged to yield and pay the toll; whereupon the Gooroo, who was very fond of money, as moft old gentlemen are, pulled fuch a long face that the collector, adding infult to injury, burft into a rude horfe-laugh when the five fanams had to be difburfed. Indignant, but helplefs, yet groaning heavily, the Gooroo exclaimed bitterly, " What do I want with a horse? If I travel as I did before I shall not be exposed to these painful trials, nor to such frightful expenses." Noodle, and Doodle, Wiseacre, Foozle, and Zany all tried to comfort him, inveighing against the vexations and dead robbery which they had just experienced; and then they once more continued their route in silence, as men do who have just been subjected to a severe mortification, till they arrived at a choultry situated at some distance from the toll-gate, where the Gooroo dismounted to rest for a while.

Here he met a traveller, with whom he entered into conversation, and related to him the crying injustice of which he had been the victim, under the pretext of exacting a toll.

" I never mounted a horse before from the day that I was born! Now to-day I have been riding for the first time, and shamefully have I been made to pay for it. The people hitherto have testified no sympathy with us, or thought of interfering in our behalf when we wanted help; but to-day they even used violence to plunder quiet inoffensive travellers of their money! Money obtained in such a way, how shall it profit them! May the vital fires its loss deprives me of, through want of the necessary sustenance and nourishment I must in consequence forego, and which those five fanams would have furnished abundantly, consume them as burning coals! Shall he who but tastes of *amoordam,* the pure drink of the gods, all but perish;

whilſt he who drinks deep of the poiſon of the world, and revels in the plunder of his fellows, prosper! Does not the poet ſay, 'They who reach the feet of Him who nouriſheth the opening flower ſhall flouriſh!' What! am I then to be thus treated! Am I not a Gooroo; and is no respeᶜt due to my calling, or to my office of inſtruᶜtor and comforter!"

After the Gooroo had diſcharged his bile in theſe bitter complaints, the traveller replied in his turn, and ſtrove to conſole him by the precepts of philoſophy.

"Ah! moſt honoured Gooroo," he ſaid, "what high morality you preach! One ſees by your diſ-courſe how the diſcharge of your pious duties and deep ſtudies have eſtranged you from the world, its vices, and its vanities. You were not born to live in this age of iron, this *Kali-yoogum* of the world, in which might overcomes right, and all things have degenerated. Vice ſtalks about triumphant on the earth; honeſty and virtue are but recolleᶜtions of the paſt; money is both the honeſty and virtue of our age! Get money, honeſtly if you can; but anyhow, get money, is the teaching of the ſchools. Money is men's Gooroo; money their caſte and their family; money is their god! Of old it was ſaid, 'Name but money, and a corpſe will open its mouth and ſay: "Money! money! Give it to me."'

"This age of Iron, honoured ſir, is an age of gold; and men honour the god whom they worſhip ſo much, that nothing is done, nothing is ſaid, but what money commands. 'Without money,' it is written, 'even the brighteft intellect will be abforbed and deftroyed by carking care for butter and falt, for oil and rice, for raiment and wood.'"

"True, true," put in the Gooro; "your words are words of wifdom. Men will do anything for gold; and, even if buried in the filthieft of mire, dainty fingers will not be found wanting to pluck it out; aye, even, too, if no other way remained, the prettieft of lips would think it no fhame or degradation to ftoop to do the act bodily with their mouths. Men and women too will eat dirt for money!"

"No doubt of it," faid the traveller, "as I can fhow from a tale which was told me in the far Weft, which I will now repeat if you, honoured fir, will liften.

"Once upon a time there was a great and mighty monarch, whofe rule extended over the whole of the Weft like that of the great Zingis over the whole of the Eaft. He loved money beyond all things, and having taxed all his nations to the utmoft, yet ftill craving for more money, there was nothing elfe left for him to tax, but what the neceffity of our nature fhould have kept exempt from fuch an impoft. His fon expoftulated in vain, urging that fuch money would ftink in men's noftrils; but the great and mighty ruler of one half of the world was not to be put afide from his purpofe, and the tax was levied. A few days after, he fent for his fon, and, whilft they were dif-cussing the affairs of state, drew forth a bag of shining golden coin, which he handed to him, saying, 'Smell it, my son; is there not an ill flavour about that money?'—'None,' replied the son, 'that I can detect; it is but fresh minted, and very pure.'—'Yet,' added

that mighty ruler, 'it is the produce of the tax, and what you said would stink in men's nostrils. Be sure, my son, it is sufficient that the money comes; trouble not yourself how or whence.'"

The Gooroo and the traveller went on chatting together for some time, until the former, perceiving that it was getting late, and wishing to profit by the coolness of the evening to continue his route, remounted his horse, and set out, accompanied, as

before, by his five disciples.   They arrived in the
first watch of the night, by sunset, at a village where
they wished to pass the night, and forgetting to tether
the horse, left him to roam and graze at will in the
surrounding lanes; but in the morning, when they
were ready to resume their journey, he was nowhere
to be found.   Wiseacre went out in search of him,
but after being absent some time, returned alone.
Dismayed and frightened at this new trouble, Noodle
and Doodle, Zany and Foozle, at once declared their
willingness to assist Wiseacre in looking for the run-
away, and they hurried out looking on all sides, but
could find no trace of him.   At last they heard that

a stray horse had been found grazing in a farmer's
meadow, and that the owner of the field, in a rage, had

locked him up, and declared that he should not be given up without a good round ransom. The Gooroo and his disciples hastened to claim their property, but the farmer obstinately refused to listen to them, saying that the horse had ranged about all the thirty half-hours of the night watches in his fields, trampling down his young growing grain, and that the damage done to his crops was more than the beast was worth; so if they would not make good the injury, he should keep the horse as a poor compensation for the losses he had sustained. Much vexed and annoyed the Gooroo went to the chief of the village, and having told him of the farmer's conduct, partly by entreaties and partly by threats, the latter consented to adjust the matter by allowing proper persons to estimate the damage done at a fair and reasonable rate, and when that had been ascertained and paid, to give up the horse. The arbitrators, having examined the fields, declared that what with breaking down, trampling down, and grazing, the loss amounted in money to some *ten** fanams; but out of respect for the rank of the Gooroo, and considering the loss and expenses to which he had already been subjected because of the horse, they would lay the damage at *four* fanams, which they ordered him to pay then and there.

When the horse was restored to him, the Gooroo

* See note on the number *ten*, as used in the second story. *Four* is used in the same way to indicate an indefinite number.

was still much put out, and, turning to his disciples, said moodily, " Since I have had this unlucky horse, my children, I am pursued by all sorts of degradation, sorrow, and expense, ill-befitting my dignity. I will ride no more, but will travel, as I did before, on foot."

With one voice Noodle and Doodle, and the other pupils, as well as the villagers, all exclaimed against such a resolve, and prayed him not to think of it. " To travel on foot," they said, " was not consistent with his high dignity. Besides, he was too much advanced in years to sustain the fatigues of a long journey, and it was absolutely necessary that he should keep the horse."

It so happened that whilst all this was passing a certain Valloovan, who had been listening all the while, approached the Gooroo, and having imposed silence upon everybody addressed him, saying, " If you will honour me with your confidence, sir, I can relieve you from all annoyance, and remove the cause of your misfortunes. After what I have heard, I have no doubt but that your horse has been bewitched by one of your secret enemies. His wicked spell is the sole cause of all the mishaps that have followed your possession of the animal; and if the demon is not quickly dispelled, he will become still more spiteful; but if you like to give me five fanams, the last and only expense you will have, I will for that moderate sum undertake to deliver your horse from the spell, and you will have nothing more to fear."

The Gooroo, though ill-inclined to incur fresh expenses, yielded to the advice of Noodle, Doodle, and Wiseacre, who, reflecting that "if one fears expense, business cannot be done," urged him to give the money, and told the magician to overcome the spell. The Valloovan, having gravely pocketed the cash, took a sight of the horse, walking round it several times, making all the while dreadful contortions and grimaces. Then with wild cries he performed his ceremonies, plucked green leaves, and sprinkled them over the back of the animal, screaming out, "*Moona! Moona! ah! oh! om!*" and other strange cabalistic words. At last, after having exhausted himself in a kind of passionate frenzy, he suddenly stopped, and regarded the horse with a pensive air. Then he patted and stroked the poor creature, and having gently rubbed its remaining ear several times, he turned quickly to the spectators, who had observed a respectful silence, and exclaimed in a transport of joy: "I have discovered the spell! It is seated in this orifice, and to charm it away we must cut off the ear quite close to the head." Then giving orders for a deep hole to be dug at some distance to bury the member with the evil spell, he took a sickle, and making it very sharp, approached the horse, bound it, and cutting off the ear as if with a razor, instantly picked it up, and running with all his speed, he threw it into the hole, and covered it well up with earth, so that the evil spell should not escape, and attach itself to any other object.

The next morning the Gooroo remounted his poor mutilated fteed; but fatigued and put out by fo many trials, inftead of continuing his journey, he retraced his fteps to the mattam, where he arrived in due time without any further accident.

STORY THE SIXTH.

THE PROPHECY OF POORAHITA, THE BRAHMAN.

The Gooroo's homily on humility; ftable-building; the example of
Kalidafa, how to lop the branches; the Poorahita and his Shafter:
"Asanam fhitam jivana nafham—cold in the rear when death is near."

RRIVED at the mattam, the
Gooroo was quite out of forts
with the world in general,
and with himfelf and his difciples, and with the horfe in
particular. Nothing feemed
to go right, and the misfortunes and accidents of his
recent journey on horfeback
haunted him day and
night. He could get
no reft. "Ah!" faid
he to himfelf, "was I not at the height
of happinefs in this world before the gift
of that unlucky fteed! How rejoiced I
was when it was prefented to me! It
seemed the fruition of all my long-
cherifhed hopes; the greateft boon that could then
add to my felicity! But how fleeting and vain! In it

I now fee only a fource of annoyance and vexation, of
forrow and trouble, and never have I fuffered fuch
mifery as has fince then fallen to my lot.   Hope is the
waking man's dream ; it is a good breakfaft, but a
bad fupper !"

Do what he would, the phantom was always prefent
to his mind ; and harping and harping upon his woes,
he loft his appetite with his fleep, till his difciples faw
him fading away like fnow in the fummer's fun ; when
one day he affembled them all together in the outer
court of the mattam, and thus addreffed them, mourn-
fully, but with fage and wife counfels, as was his wont ;
for the good Gooroo Simple never loft the opportunity
of improving an occafion, and great was confequently
the privilege of thofe who enjoyed his fociety.   The
fubject he had at heart was, how to difpofe of the
horfe, and that was, as it were, to form the text of his
difcourfe ; but, like many other texts, it was but a peg
to hang notes upon.   So he began :—

" My beloved children, as I advance in life, day by
day am I more and more convinced that the pleafures of this world are all vanity, and vanity will prove
but vexation in the end.   The world's pleafures are
falfe pleafures.   Good unmixed with evil, fweets unmixed with bitters, or joy unmixed with forrow, are
each here not attainable.   The fun fhines but to caufe
the rain to fall; happinefs is the fure forerunner of
tears.   Yet we muft be content, for is it not written,
' The world is within him who underftands the way of

five things : of tafte, of light, of touch, of found, of fmell.' "

The gift horfe, it is true, was a very miferable and unfound beaft; fo the Gooroo reflected with fomething like fatisfaction that it had coft him nothing, and that as no fanam nor kafhoo had been paid for it, he could part with it without the leaft regret ; fo he continued his difcourfe, faying :—

" This very day I am more fully aware than ever I was before, how futile a thing it is to hope to find a rofe without a thorn ; to fet one's affections upon that

I

which may fade ; to be sure of the enjoyment of any anticipated pleafure.   Hem ! Alas ! does not our own experience prove this?   When the horfe was pre-fented to me by the civility of a firanger, without fee or reward, what joy could equal mine ! What antici-pation of pleafure furpafs that which rofe up within me !   I imagined that I had little more to defire in this world ; yet how vain my hopes !   You yourfelves were witnefles of the fad misfortunes which followed in fuch quick fucceflion, even on the very day when the piece of good fortune fell to my lot.   Muft we then fwallow fo much bitternefs with every fingle drop of honey !   Alas, that it fhould be fo ! but there is no grain of rice without its hufk, no plum without a ftone, no fruit without a tafielefs fkin, and in two cabs of dates there is one cab of ftones and more.   There is much evil mingled with the good which is found in the world !   All this is indeed true ; yet the evils which I endured within the fpace of that one day were great in the extreme.   I have thought long and carefully as to what caufe to attribute them, and I can find no other than the gift of the horfe, which I received with fo much joy.   I was not born to ride about in fuch ftate and dignity.   ' Be humble, be courteous,' fays the poet ; for without thefe of what avail are other qualities ?'   Why, then, did I ftep out of the path I was to tread ?   The gods have punifhed my vanity by the gift of a horfe, which has occafioned all my troubles.   Shall I then place my will in oppo-

fition to my deftiny? I, who up to this time have led
a retired and unobtrufive life; what, at its clofe, have
I to do with the world's pomps and vanities? No,
no, let me be humble, as befits my calling. Is not
virtue the greateft gain, and its neglect the greateft
lofs? Let me part with the horfe; let it be fent back
to its former owner."

Noodle and Doodle, who had liftened with breath-
lefs and devoted attention, as had alfo Wifeacre,
Foozle, and Zany, to the eloquent and touching difcourfe of their honoured mafter, both broke out at
once with the words, "No, no, fir; indeed, indeed,
this muft not be!" "Confider," added Wifeacre,
"whofe gift the horfe was, and how it was fent to you
in the hour of great need. The ftranger who fo
kindly entertained us in his houfe was but the inftrument; the gift was from the gods. Is it a horfe
which you yourfelf felected, a horfe which you yourfelf paid for? No, you had no idea of doing either
the one or the other; and the fhadow of the terra-
cotta horfe was caft upon the furface of the refervoir
as a type of the living one, which the traveller was at
hand to prefent you with. Do not talk, then, of
parting with the good the gods have fent you.
The horfe came of itfelf, without feeking on our part.
Who can fail to trace the hand that gave it? To
fend it back will, then, be in direct oppofition to the
will of the gods; will be an act of impiety and dif-
obedience; will be a great and crying fin; and cannot

fail to bring misfortune for the future upon your head and upon ours. Is not ingratitude the greateſt of all ſin? Are we not told that 'life may yet be his who has obliterated all other virtues; but that from him who blots out the remembrance of benefits received, life has ſurely departed?'

" No, ſir; indeed, indeed, this muſt not be. Beſides, ſir, what has happened, has happened, and what ſhall be, will be! Then, too, has not the Valloovan caſt out the ſpirit of miſchief which dwelt in the horſe's ear; and have we not buried it, along with the ear itſelf, afar off from hence, ſo as to keep it from doing us further harm?"

" Indeed, indeed, ſir," chimed in Zany and Foozle, "this muſt not be; the horſe muſt not be ſent back again to its former owner. There muſt be a beginning, even as A is the firſt letter of the alphabet."

" In my own city my name, in a ſtrange city my clothes, procure me reſpect," ſaid a ſage of old. So when the Gooroo had liſtened attentively to the rea-ſoning of Wiſeacre, he ſaid to himſelf, " If a man keeps a horſe, his neighbours know full well what kind of a horſe it is; but away from them one horſe is as good as another; and the world merely ſays he keeps his horſe." Other like thoughts, too, roſe in his mind at the ſame time, and after a little while he turned round to his diſciples and ſaid :—

" Be it then according as you deſire; for I would not act in any way contrary to what you have proved to be fo manifeftly the will of the gods. However, in order that the fame misfortune which happened the other day may not occur again, and caufe us frefh trouble and expenfe, it will not do to turn the horfe out at night, but he muft be kept tied up in the mattam, but where I do not know; fo take counfel together, and arrange where his ftable fhall be, where he can remain in comfort, fcreened from the cold winds at night and from the fcorching rays of the fun by day."

"Sir," faid Wifeacre, "if that is all that is required, there is but little need of taking counfel together. If Noodle and Doodle, Zany and Foozle, will but each lend a hand, it fhall be done in a trice; and in yonder corner of the mattam as pretty a ftable as you can wifh, fhall be erected before the firft watch of the night." So faying, without more ado he girded him-felf with a rope round the loins, and fnatching up a hatchet and a bill-hook, ftarted off to the roadfide, where there ftood a large banian-tree, about a hun-dred yards from the mattam. Arrived there, he foon climbed half-way up the tree, and felecting a large branch, which hung horizontally over the road, he fat himfelf aftride it, with his face turned to the ftem of the tree, and began to chop luftily away with his hatchet at that part of the branch that was between his own trunk and that of the tree, not aware that when it fhould fall, he, too, muft of neceffity fall with it.

Whilft he was fo engaged, it chanced that a
Brahman, a learned pundit, a *Poorahita* well-fkilled
in aftrology and the reading of the ftars, was on his

way to prefide over a village feftival not far from the
mattam of the Gooroo Simple, and to tell the people

their fortunes. Seeing the perilous pofition of Wife-acre, and being of a kind and charitable nature, he called out to him: " Hallo, brother ! What, in the name of common fenfe, are you doing there? Pray change your pofition, or when the branch breaks away from the ftem, it will bring you to the ground with it, and you may chance to break your neck."

" Bird of ill-omen," replied Wifeacre, " why do you come here prophecying evil to me? Begone with your evil bodings, and take that for remembrance;" faying which he unfheathed the long pointed knife which he carried at his waift, and aiming at the Brahman's face, fent it towards him with great force ; but the latter, thinking the young man either mad or a fool, ducked his head, and let the knife fly over it, faying, " Why fhould I interfere? If he is fool enough to break his neck, let him; I'm not refpon-fible for it."

This little epifode only made Wifeacre chop away more vigoroufly. His blood boiled at what he looked upon as an infult. Whack went the hatchet—whack, whack ! When he had got half through the wood, crack, crack, crack, and fnap—down came the branch, and, as the *Poorahita* had predicted, down came Wife-acre with it, emitting a found from his head much like that of a water-cafk, when there is no water in it. It was fortunate that he fell upon his head, or he might have broken a limb. As it was, though a little ftunned, he foon recovered himfelf, and picking

himſelf up, and rubbing his head, he exclaimed:
" *Am! am! ma!* Lackaday! that Brahman is a great
Shaſtri, a wiſe *Poorahita*, a wonderful prophet! Juſt as
he predicted, ſo it has happened unto me!" So ſaying,
he ſtarted upon his legs, and commenced running in
the direction the aſtrologer had taken; for the latter
was already at a conſiderable diſtance from the ſpot
upon which Wiſeacre had fallen.

Seeing him thus rapidly gaining ground upon him,
the *Poorahita* was ſomewhat terrified, and ſaid to
himſelf, " What can that wild beaſt want with me?
He has already tried to do me an injury by throwing
his knife at my head; perhaps he may now ſtrive to
murder me outright." But his fears abated, for as
Wiſeacre approached him, within ſpeaking diſtance,
he joined both hands together, and raiſing them up
to his forehead, bowed his head reſpectfully as he
made the cuſtomary *namaſcara*, or obeiſance to a
Brahman.

" Accept, I pray you," ſaid Wiſeacre, " my moſt
ample apologies for the neglect of the counſel you
gave me, and for the very ill return I made to your
very great kindneſs. He who can propheſy ſo cor-
rectly and ſo truly as you did but now, muſt indeed
be able to read the ſtars, and to foretel the future.
You are a great *Shaſtri*, a highly-gifted *Poorahita*.
I therefore beſeech you to grant me one boon; for, by
my own experience, I am certain you can tell me what
ſhall happen, what come to paſs. Do not deny my

requeft; I am your fervant. I am a difciple of the wife and famous Gooroo Simple, who lives at the mattam down yonder, beyond the banian-tree, from which I was fevering a limb when you foretold my fall to earth with the branch upon which I then fat aftride. My name is Wifeacre, and Noodle and Doodle, and Zany and Foozle, are my fellow-difciples. We all love our honoured mafter with the moft heartfelt affection; for he is a man of great wifdom and piety, and of the moft profound virtue and bene-ficence. No child can love his father as I love him; and as he is now very aged and infirm, I am fearful that he will die when we leaft expect it, and that his end is even already near at hand. I therefore appeal to you, to whom the future is open and known as the events of yefterday, to foothe my anxiety and to fatisfy my longing defire by revealing to me the length of time my honoured mafter has yet to live, the exact time of his departure, and the fymptoms by which I may tell the near approach of his death. Do not re-fufe my prayer; do not think my requeft too trivial to be attended to. You who could fo truly foretel my fall from the tree, can, with eafe to yourfelf, com-ply with my wifhes. I am your fervant."

So urged, what could the Brahman do? He did not want to throw away the opportunity he faw, of having his fame as a prophet fpread over the land by Wifeacre and his fellow difciples; yet he did not like to rifk his reputation upon a random anfwer; fo in the hope of effecting his escape, if an opportunity should occur, he kept giving evasive answers, till at length, finding that Wiseacre was not to be put off with them, and to rid himself of the dilemma in which the persistency of his petitioner had placed him, he turned round to him at length, and said :—

" Listen attentively to what I read in language of the stars," and then added, in flow and solemn cadence : " '*Asanam shitam, jivana nasham;*' when that sentence is fulfilled, then you may look for the period when Dharma shall take your honoured Gooroo from you."

" 'Tis an unknown tongue to me," said Wiseacre. " *Asanam shitam* is euphonious, and so is *jivana nasham;* but the sound conveys to me no sense; I pray you therefore interpret to me this unknown tongue, this language of the fringes of eternity, of the spheres whence spirits speak to mortals in the world below."

" It is," replied the Brahman, " the mystic language of the initiated, which none others may comprehend ; but it implies here, " *cold in the rear, when death is near,*" because the heat of the body being longest retained about the heart, the lower extremities first become cold and paralysed, and consequently these words indicate the success of Dharma's flank movement upon the rear, prior to his final attack upon the citadel of life."

" *Asanam shitam, jivana nasham*—cold in the rear,

when death is near," repeated Wiseacre; and making again a moft profound *namafcara* to the *Poorahita*, he received his *affirvahdam*, his bow of difmiflal, and

left the prefence of the great aftrologer, well fatisfied with the reception he had received, no lefs than with the information he had gained. Arrived at the banian-tree, repeating all the way, left he fhould forget them, the myftic words, *Afanam fhitam, jivana nafham,* he felected as much of the wood as would ferve his purpofe; and having uncoiled the rope from his loins, and attached it to the loofe branches, he dragged them along the road to the mattam, pondering upon the wifdom and found fenfe of the *Poorahita*, and muttering half unconfcioufly to himfelf, *cold in the rear, when death is near.*

Arrived at the mattam, he found Noodle and Doodle, Zany and Foozle, all bufily employed in erecting the stable for the horse; so having relieved himself of his burden, and pointed out to Noodle how the branches were to be placed to form the roof of the building upon which they were engaged, he proceeded to report himself to the Gooroo, and to relate to him what had befallen him since he had left the mattam.

Bowing respectfully, with his hands raised to his forehead, as he entered the presence of the Gooroo, he said, in a solemn tone, *Asanam shitam, jivana nasham,* and again bowing reverently, held his tongue.

It seemed to the aged Gooroo as if a voice had spoken to him from the grave, and for a time neither broke the solemn silence. At length the Gooroo repeated the mystic phrase, *Asanam shitam, jivana nasham,* saying, " My son, what words are these, and whence the mysterious chill they impart?"

" Dear and honoured master," replied Wiseacre, " they are words of wisdom and counsel for our guidance; and if you will listen to me, I will tell you how I came to learn them, and why I treasure them." Hereupon he proceeded to give the Gooroo a full account of the fulfilment of the *Poorahita's* prophecy of his fall from the tree, and of the manner in which he had obtained the cabalistic words which he had just pronounced.

When Wiseacre had concluded, the Gooroo Simple desired him to call in Noodle and Doodle, Zany and Foozle, and when all were assembled together, and he had repeated to them the narrative of Wiseacre's adventure, he thus addressed them :—

"My children, the world has changed much since it was first created, and mankind not less so. In the *Sooti-yoogam* man lived for a hundred thousand years, and his stature was three times its present size. Then came the *Tirtah-yoogam*, when one-third of mankind lapsed into sin, and life was but a tenth as long as it was before, and men died at ten thousand years. Next followed the *Durapaar-yoogam*, and half the human race became depraved, when the gods shortened the life of man to a thousand years. Now, in this age of iron, this *Kali-yoogam*, life seldom reaches one hundred years, and certainty has passed away. Dharma sits down with us in the day, and is ever in the midst of us in the night.

"*Asanam shitam, jivana nasham*, are words of wisdom, words of caution; therefore, let each of us copy them down, and always carry them about with us. It is well that all should think of their latter end ;" and, oblivious for the moment, he muttered to himself, "Cold in the rear when death is near." "Well, indeed, is it to contemplate one's latter end without dismay. Now I cannot doubt that the Brahman who so accurately foretold the fate of Wiseacre is a great and wise Shastri, and that the shaster he has sent to me will also be verified. 'Cold in the rear when death is near,' is a true saying; so for the future all my feet-washing and ablutions, which are prescribed by our law, but which may bring on the evil, muſt be in abeyance. Yet I cannot wreſtle with deſtiny. What ſhall be will be; as fate has decreed, ſo let it be; for when all is ſaid, at bottom it is wiſe to be content!"

STORY THE SEVENTH.

THE FALL FROM THE HORSE.

"Money, as well as need, makes the old man trot;" the lofs of the turban, and what befell in confequence; the fall from the horfe, what the Cadjan faid, and how it was remedied; the fymptom, Afanam fhitam, cold in the rear.

N the coldeft flint, it is faid, there is hot fire, and there is life in a mufcle; and while there is life there is hope. A man is not fo foon healed as hurt; fo the Gooroo, knowing that forewarned is forearmed, avoided all things which could expedite the fulfilment of the prophecy, and, by a liberal ufe of hot fpiced difhes, curries and pillaus, peppers, ginger, and affafœtida, he contrived to keep his body tolerably warm; whilft to imprefs the importance of the words *Afanam fhitam, jivana nafham,* more ftrongly upon his difciples, he from that time never addreffed them unlefs ftanding with his back to the ftove, with his hands behind him, hoping thereby to put off the evil day predicted by the great Shaftri, the learned *Poorahita.*

For a time all went on well; but, unhappily, other confiderations began to prefs upon him, and he who had but erft railed fo eloquently againft money, had now to feel what a neceffary evil it had become. Money muft be had, fo he foon faw that it was needful that he and his difciples fhould travel round the diftrict, from village to village, to collect their dues; for it was quite clear that by ftaying in the mattam, no income could be realized. Under thefe circumftances, the Gooroo, ever forward in the path of duty, affembled his five followers, and mounted his horfe, having to perform a journey that would take fome days to accomplifh. Unfortunately, inftead of taking the direct road, and wifhing to avoid the toll, they proceeded acrofs country, and as they were all ignorant of the crofs-roads, on the following morning they had wandered fo far out of the way, that they were obliged to go back towards the mattam. The cool fhade of the banian-trees, their wide-fpreading boughs, covered with thick foliage, the largeft and loweft of which were horizontal, and from which fuckers or roots of various length depended until they reached the ground and became new trunks, formed a bewildering grove for the travellers to tra- verfe, excepting when the track was well defined.

Abforbed in thought, the Gooroo paffed on among thefe downward hanging boughs, one of which caught

his turban from his head, when it fell to the ground. Without ftopping, thinking that his difciples would pick it up as a matter of courfe, he travelled on in filence for a confiderable diftance, not deeming it neceffary to remind either of them of fuch a plain duty; while they, not having received any orders from their mafter on the fubject, left it on the fpot where it had fallen. Roufing himfelf from his reverie, the Gooroo fuddenly afked for his turban.

"Your turban," Doodle replied, "lies where you let it fall. We did not pick it up, becaufe you gave us no orders to do fo."

Juftly difpleafed, the Gooroo reproved them feverely for their thoughtlefs conduct and want of attention.

"Go quickly, and find my turban," he faid, in an angry voice; "and henceforth I order you to pick up everything that falls from the horfe."

Foozle, whofe duty as groom of the ftole it was to look after the body linen, ran fwiftly to the place where the turban lay, and taking it from the ground, returned without delay to his companions; but as he approached them, he perceived that the horfe was uneafy, probably from having fed upon the commons, where the coarfe rank grafs had been frefhened by

recent rains, fo that the poor animal was fuffering from diarrhœa. The fymptoms could not be miftaken, and remembering the order juft before given, he rufhed forward with the turban extended in his hands, intending to fecure "everything that fell from the horfe." The turban was foon filled, fo Foozle called to his mafter, faying, "Sir! fir! I pray you to ftop. Here is fomething which has fallen from the horfe, and I bring it to you conformably to your orders."

The Gooroo, thus appealed to, gracioufly drew up, and turned to receive that which Foozle brought to him; but when he faw his turban thus defiled, he was in great paffion.

"Tchy! tchy! Fie! for fhame!" he cried, angrily, and with intenfe difguft. "What have you picked up? Why have you not more fenfe? Throw it away. Begone! and wafh and purify my turban inftantly."

His difciples, aftonifhed to hear Foozle thus re-proved for having but duly obeyed his mafter's orders, replied in a tone of ill humour, "Why, fir, what has he done to difpleafe you? You were angry with us, but a moment ago, for having omitted to obey a command you had not given, and here you rebuke us through him, for having followed your orders to the letter! Did you not bid us to pick up everything that fell from the horfe?"

"Not fo," replied the Gooroo, with a ftately air; "there are fome things which it is proper to pick up, and, again, there are others which it is not proper to pick up. You fhould exercife your wits, and act like men, and not like a parcel of children."

"We are not clever enough," returned Wifeacre, "to comprehend fuch nice diftinctions. We are plain, practical people, making no pretence to wit or wifdom, and cannot underftand from fuch general terms what your precife meaning is. Such miſtakes are very difagreeable to us, and no lefs fo your anger; and in order not to be fubjeƈt to either in future, be pleafed to give us a liſt of fuch things as it is proper to pick up, fhould they happen to drop whilſt you are riding, that we may be under no doubt as to what we ought to do."

This requeſt was too fenfible for the Gooroo to difpute; fo, on the fpur of the moment, he called for a *cadjan*, or palm leaf, and a ſtyle, and wrote upon it a liſt of fuch things as it was proper for them to pick up if they fell. He then gave this liſt to Noodle, ordering him to read it aloud, from time to time, fo that all might underſtand exaƈtly what it fpecified. When this had been done, they promifed ſtriƈtly to abide by the direƈtions there fet forth, and then refumed their way in peace for fome time, glad of a little quiet after fuch unufual anger and fquabbling. Beguiling the time with inſtruƈtive remarks upon the varied objeƈts around them, they came at length to a ditch, filled with mud and water, which they were obliged to jump over. For a horfe in ordinary condition it was not a difficult place to crofs; but for one fo lame and worn out as that on which the Gooroo rode, it was too great an effort; befides, the ground was wet and ſlippery; and as he went tottering down the bank his foot fank in the mud, from which he could not extricate it, fo that he ſtumbled and fell on his fide, and caſt his rider headlong into the mire.

There the poor Gooroo lay extended at full length on his back, but fo embedded in the mud, that with every effort he made to raife himfelf, he only fank deeper into it. Noodle and Doodle, Wifeacre, Zany, and Foozle, feeing the horfe ftruggle violently to extricate itfelf, while their mafter lay perfectly ftill, concluded that the horfe was fuffering the moft, and ought therefore to be the firft fuccoured ; fo they fet to work, and having drawn him out of the ditch, they returned to the Gooroo. Impatient, and angry at being left fo long in the mire, he called loudly for their affiftance, and defired them to lift him out quickly. But with grave looks they ftood around him, and Noodle, opening a fmall travelling-bag which he carried, took out of it the *cadjan* leaf, with the lift of things to be picked up fhould they fall from the horfe, and fhaking his head forrowfully, cautioned Doodle and Foozle, Wifeacre and Zany, one after another, as to the different objects exprefsly ftated, reading, as he did fo, aloud to them from the order :

" You muft pick up my turban if it falls ; fo, too, my waift cloth, or the cloth which covers my head and fhoulders ;—in a word, if any other veftment, or any other object which I carry on my perfon, falls, you muft pick it up."

The five difciples, complying literally with the tenor of the document, all fhaking their heads folemnly, proceeded to ftrip the Gooroo, piece by piece, of each of his garments, leaving him like a new-

born babe, entirely deſtitute of clothing. The poor
old man ſaw them depart in amazement, and hurriedly
calling them back, told them to raiſe him, as he was
too weak to help himſelf; but his diſciples poſitively
refuſed to do ſo, ſaying that his name was not to be
found in the liſt, and, having his written inſtructions,
they were pledged to obey them, and them only.   The
Gooroo, thus ſorely tried, uſed prayers and threats to
vanquiſh their obſtinacy, but all in vain; they refuſed
to liſten to his entreaties, and to juſtify their refuſal,
produced the document again, ſaying, " Behold your
orders; read this liſt of articles, to which we have
ſtrictly conformed. If you had deſired to be picked
up yourſelf, ſhould you fall from the horſe, it ſhould
have been written down with the reſt; not appearing
on the cadjan, we ſhould be acting contrary to your
expreſs commands, and ſhould be liable to your diſ-
pleaſure and fierce rebukes, if we raiſed you up out of
the ditch. You have already been angry with us
twice to-day under circumſtances wherein we erred
ignorantly; but we will not a third time run the riſk of
offending you upon a ſubject where, having your full
written inſtructions what to do, the blame would reſt
wholly on ourſelves if we varied from them."

   The Gooro, aware that his pupils would not liſten
to reaſon, and that they would leave him fixed in the
mud, from which he tried in vain to extricate himſelf,
deſired them to give him the cadjan and ſtyle, and
added at the end of the liſt, in large letters: " *And if*

the Gooroo Simple, your mafter, happens to fall, it is moft proper that you pick him up firft of all."

Of courfe, after that, not a word could be faid in objection, and no more difficulty exifted. They took their poor old mafter into their arms, and carried him away from the ditch; and as the rear of his perfon from head to foot was covered with mud, they took him to a pond that was near, and having wafhed him, as well as his clothes, in the cold water, they dreffed him again, without giving the latter time to dry. Once more he mounted his horfe, and finding the road, they all returned to the mattam, where they arrived worn out with their march acrofs fields and uncultivated waftes, and the Gooroo fell ferioufly ill from his fall and the events which followed it.

STORY THE EIGHTH.

THE PROPHECY FULFILLED.

The terrors of Afanam fhitam; the Gooroo orders his own grave; Mr.
Merriman, Afangadan, the fon of "Old Fog," Achedanamoorti, brings
confolation; the rice-beater Poojei, a novel facrifice to the gods; the
ftory of the Chitty's pretty wife and the Pandarams; a good ftory
better than phyfic, and a good breakfaft better than a grand funeral;
Afanam fhitam not to be explained away; jivana nafham follows;
lying in ftate; purification of the dead, and funeral of the Gooroo
Simple.

LL indeed was the poor old man when Foozle waited upon him the next morning with the change of linen his enforced bath of yefterday had neceffitated. Strange, though each of his disciples always carried about with him, fince the day it had been received, the myfterious

fhafter of the Brahman, whilft the Gooroo fat in the cold water of the pond, not one of them recol-

lected the words, *Afanam fhitam, jivana nafham!*
Indeed, it was only after he had again mounted
his horfe, and the wet garments intercepted the
warmth of the faddle-cloth, that the old man himfelf fuddenly called to mind the evident import of
them, as he fat fhivering in the cold. He could not
miftake the rapidity of the fpread of the chill which
pervaded him upwards from his feet, till it feemed to
fix itfelf, as it were, between him and the faddle upon
which he rode. As the cold increafed, he at firft fought
comfort in the recollection of the warmth of the
mattam, faying to himfelf, " Is it not written, ' If thou
haft increafed thy water, thou muft alfo increafe thy
meal ;' I will have fomething to comfort me and
warm me when I get home." But " there is no
medicine againft death," and as his thoughts wandered
imperceptibly towards the mattam and its comforts,
there fuddenly came upon him the fame unearthly
chill, which he had experienced when Wifeacre firft
repeated to him the cabaliftic prophecy of the *Poorahita.* The Gooroo grew fad and forrowful, neverthelefs he kept his thoughts to himfelf; but the proceffion feemed to him like that of his own funeral.

Arrived at the mattam, he felt fick and unwell from
the effects of the cold and his fall, but attributing his
fufferings only to the near approach of the fulfilment
of the prophecy, he retired fafting to bed, only to become colder and colder, toffing reftlefsly about all
night without obtaining a fingle wink of fleep, fo that

when day broke, though "the sun rose, the disease did not abate," as the words of wisdom have often foretold; for in his case they were not to be fulfilled.

When Foozle approached the bed upon which his beloved master lay, he was greatly alarmed to perceive that his countenance was changed, his eyes sunk in their sockets, whilst a raging fire seemed to light up the sunken orbs; that his face, withered and shrivelled, had an unearthly hue, a brownish tint in places making the ghastly paleness more defined; and that his mouth was parched, his lips colourless, and his words confused and indistinct; whilst he stared at him as it were upon vacancy, scarcely conscious of his presence.

It was the custom of the mattam that after the morning ablutions, Noodle and Doodle, Zany, Foozle and Wiseacre should all assemble round the Gooroo, and partake together of the boiled rice and tyer which served for the frugal breakfast of the venerable man and his disciples. When Foozle had summoned his four companions, they were equally alarmed at the change which a single night had brought about in the appearance of the Gooroo. How different from the calm dignified countenance which they were wont to behold; from the gentle and kindly greeting which met each as he approached; from the cheerful smile which made them all feel welcome!

Calling them all around his bed, the old man rose up, and speaking in a sepulchral tone, as he stretched forth his withered arms and blessed them, added, " My beloved children, the hour of my death is at hand. Prepare, therefore, that which is neceſſary, that my body may ſpeedily have its ſepulture, for I have not many minutes to live."

With tears in their eyes, they all beſought him to tell them how in a ſingle night ſuch misfortune had come upon them. "Tell us, we pray thee," ſaid Noodle, ſobbing, whilſt the tears fell faſt down his face, "tell us, we pray thee, what has happened, and how we may avert ſo great an evil;" and the ſobs and tears of his diſciples told that the ſorrow they expreſſed was heartfelt, and that there was not a trace in any one of them of the angry feeling of yeſterday.

The good old man was ſenſibly touched, and it was ſome moments before he could give utterance to the words :—

"My children, have you ſo ſoon forgotten the words, *Aſanam ſhitam, jivana naſham?* That time is now come; 'Cold in the rear, when death is near.' In the ditch into which I was caſt when the horſe fell, there was much mud and water, and as I ſat up ſtriving to extricate myſelf a chill pervaded the whole portion of my body from the hips downwards. In my extremity, and anxious only to get out of the ditch, I was not ſtruck by the verification of the ſhaſter, nor did it occur to me when you placed me upon my back in the cold water of the pond; but when I had again mounted the horſe I could no longer conceal from myſelf how cold, how icy cold, was that part of the body which the prophecy fo clearly indicated fhould, by its chill, announce to me the approach of Dharma. I, therefore, would not ftruggle with fate, but retired at once to my bed to contemplate my latter end ; and during the night the bodily pains and uneafinefs I have experienced, and the continued chill which affected the part I have named, and which even now has not a fingle particle of warmth in it, has made me fully fenfible that my hour is come ; and that my laft moment is at hand. It is needlefs to deliberate ; to doubt is wafte of time ; the prophecy is fulfilled ! Go, therefore, and prepare all things that are neceffary for my interment."

The Gooroo was a long while in delivering thefe words to his pupils. He was in much pain from the fall and bruifes of yefterday, and his fpirit groaned in bitternefs within him. At times he ftopped and moaned ; at times, too, he muttered to himfelf, half unconfcioufly, " Cold in the rear, when death is near." When he had finifhed, his difciples, as was their wont, were for fome time loft in contemplation, and no one broke the filence. At length Noodle, who, like the other four, could not but fee how clofely the ftate of the Gooroo's body coincided with the words of the fhafter, and was greatly terrified, endeavoured by a ftrong effort to overcome his own fears, that he might tranquillize the mind of his beloved mafter by words of confolation which imparted none to himfelf, and faid :—

" 'My honoured mafter, you are exhaufted for want of food. We have here both tyer and rice prepared for the morning's meal, and frefh milk and pepper water. 'A cheerful mind, peace, and fimple diet,' are the beft and trueft medicines. Difmifs the thought of death, and ftrive to overcome the evil forebodings which the accident of yefterday has conjured up. 'Who goes to bed fupperlefs, fhall tumble and tofs.' Partake with us of the morning's meal, and all will yet be well;" and much more to the fame purport was uttered by Wifeacre, Doodle, Zany, and Foozle, but all to no purpofe; for fo imbued was the Gooroo with the words of the fhafter, the fulfilment of which he looked upon as near at hand, that he did not appear to hear thofe they addreffed to him, but continued to moan and groan, uttering to himfelf in an under tone, *Afanam fhitam, jivana nafham.*

Finding all their efforts of no avail, Wifeacre confulted his coufin Merriman, whom the people in the village called *Afangadan*, becaufe of his love of chaffing and buffoonery. He was the fon of old Fog, as the villagers had nicknamed *Achedanamoorti*, the late chief of the village, for fhort, and was a man much beloved by them, no lefs than an old friend of the Gooroo Simple. Indeed, it was through him, who was many years his fenior, that Wifeacre was firft introduced to the latter. Go where he would, Merriman was a favourite. He was full of quips and quiddities, wife faws and wondrous fentences, and could elicit a joke

out of the dulleſt materials. Knowing how great an
influence Merriman could exerciſe over the Gooroo,
Wiſeacre had been aſked by his fellow-diſciples to
prevail upon his couſin to come and ſee their beloved
maſter, as, beſides his jovial diſpoſition, he was famous
for caſting out megrims and evil ſpirits, blue devils
and the mumps. In fact, he was the ſorcerer of the
village, its augur and prophet.

Now, when he had heard all that Wiſeacre had to
tell about the ſtrange malady of his old friend, he
haſtened with him to the mattam, and putting on a
half-ſerious and half-comic expreſſion of countenance,
as he entered, he exclaimed, " How now, old boy !

what ails you? what has come over the fpirit of your dream?" but feeing that the Gooroo was not then inclined to jeft, he added, in a more ferious tone, "Tell me, my father, my honoured friend, my Gooroo, what is this forrow, what this grief, that I may find means to comfort and uphold you?"

But to all his advances, the Gooroo merely groaned out the words, "*Afanam fhitam, jivana nafham,*—cold in the rear, when death is near!" Seeing that neither banter nor ferious talk was of any avail, Merriman gave into the vein of the fick man's thoughts, and faid :—

"True, the prophecy of the Poorahita muft come to pafs; but I can avert it from you, and caft it back upon himfelf. I can turn cold into heat by performing the rice-beater *Poojei;* drive the cold out of you, and make it defcend upon him rearward as heat, fo that he fhall not be able to fleep by night or by day, nor to fit down to reft his weary limbs, for the very heat in his rear. Tell me his name. Tell me who he is, and where to find him, that I may at once remove this malady from you, and confume him with heat from the rice-beater *Poojei.*"

The Gooroo had liftened attentively to the words of Merriman. "Tell me," faid he, in a flow, fepulchral tone, "what is this *Poojei,* this facrifice, of which you fpeak? I am defirous of knowledge, and even now, when I feel life flitting away, I cannot reft till I learn what this is; for I, who have joined in all the many

Poojeis of the temple, never heard of this rice-beater *Poojei.*"

" It is not to be wondered at," replied Merriman, " that you, my dear Gooroo, should never have heard of the rice-beater *Poojei*. It is but seldom that it can be properly performed; for it requires a combination no lefs of inner than of outer qualities in the fame perfon, which the great fhafiri, Buddha, himfelf but rarely met with; and, indeed, it is a *Poojei*, which needs neither muficians nor dancing-girls to ftir up the paffions of thofe who take part in it, and fo is but little heard of amongft the inner *Oodfameiyams* and outer *Poorrachchameiyans*, whofe *Poojei* fervice, like the myfteries of the wifeft people of the Weft, whom men called *Athenaioi*, may not be told to any but the initiated. Still, as far as I may tell what kind of *Poojei* this is of which you would know, if you will liften attentively, you may learn from the following tale :—

" There was once a certain *chitty*, a merchant, a follower of the goddefs Shivan, whom he worfhipped as the protector of commerce, and the propitiator of his own particular fuccefs in trade. As the goddefs had fmiled upon him, he delighted to feed at his table the *Pandarams*, the mendicant penitent priefts of Shivan, afking them to his houfe whenever he met them in his way to or from the bazaar; for he recollected the words of the poet, " Home and its comforts are ours, but in truft to exercife hofpitality ?"

Now this rich *chitty* had a young and pretty wife, whom he had taken to himfelf in his old age, and having no children, fhe ruled her hufband pretty well in all other matters excepting in this, which he called " pious hofpitality." He had a great defire to hear himfelf called father by a merry group of joyous boys and girls, and, by thus propitiating the goddefs and her priefts, he hoped, in fome meafure, by the fanctity and prayers of the latter, that this wifh of his heart might yet be gratified. The *Pandarams*, fingularly enough, by fome accident or other, feemed to congregate right in the path of the *chitty*, juft at the hours of his going to, or returning from, the bazaar; and as he never paffed by any one of them without afking him to his table, you may be fure that he feldom had any unoccupied feats to fpare. However, many or few, he treated them always with hofpitality, and never difmiffed them without a more fubftantial evidence of his refpect and goodwill. Once in the way this might have been pleafant enough, but when it occurred every day, the *chitty's* young and pretty wife began to tire of the extra labour which fell to her fhare in confequence; for what with preparing the rice, dreffing curries and pillaus, and making cakes and paftry, all the days of her life were fpent over the hot ftoves in the kitchen. Being young and pretty, you will perhaps fay what could have been eafier than afferting her authority, and forbidding her hufband to invite any more of thefe unwelcome guefts? Softly;

she had not been married quite long enough for that; besides, she had well studied her husband's peculiarities, and knew for certain that if she openly opposed his wishes, he would only the more strenuously insist upon having them complied with. But who ever knew her mother wit fail her, when a woman has a point to carry!

What she could not do openly, she could manage by stratagem; besides, though she could have told some pretty tales, had she been so disposed, of the chastity and sanctity of these holy *Pandarams,* she was but a single woman against a whole host of long-visaged, cadaverous-looking, sanctimonious, and hungry priests, who would not be lightly driven from the flesh-pots of the credulous old *chitty,* any more than flies from a newly-opened jar of honey. So to put an end to her drudgery, she hit upon a most ingenious stratagem, as you will find.

" The next morning her husband had scarcely left his own door, when he was accosted by a *Pandaram,* who requested alms.

" ' At this moment,' said the *chitty,* ' I am too busy to attend suitably to your request; but when I have transacted the business which presses, at the bazaar, I will return home, and give it my best attention. In the meantime, go to my house, and tell my wife that I have asked you to await my return there, and to partake of tiffin with me. She will know what I mean, and will do everything in conformity to my wifhes. Our humble home is often honoured by fuch vifits of holy men.'

"The *Pandaram*, nothing loth, betook himfelf at once to the houfe of the merchant, where the lady met him with honeyed words and finiles, luring him into the toils fhe was already preparing in her mind, through means of which, for the future, he fhould ferve as a warning to the whole fanctimonious fraternity which infefted her houfe. Seeing at once that he was a perfect ftranger, and had never been her hufband's gueft before, fhe faid :—

" ' I am delighted with this kind vifit ;' and fpreading a mat on the houfe-bench, fhe added, " Pray be feated, fir ; it will not be long before my hufband returns from the bazaar." No fooner was the *Pandaram* feated, than fhe quickly proceeded to fweep out the court thoroughly ; which having done, fhe removed all further defilements by fprinkling the ground with water with which the frefh and fragrant depofit from the cow had been well mixed, the rich perfume of which was grateful to the noftrils of the holy man. When thefe arrangements were completed, fhe purified her hands and feet, wafhed her face, put fandal-pafte on her forehead, and powdered her arms and fhoulders with faffron. The *Pandaram* looked curioufly on to fee what all this was to lead to, and was loft in aftonifhment when he faw her bring one of the two rice-beaters from the end of the court with much folemnity, rub firft it, and then herfelf with afhes, till the black

ebony appeared white, and her hands and arms ca-
daverous; and placing it in the middle of the court,
proſtrate herſelf three times in front of it, chanting:

'Home and its comforts are both, in reality,
Given in truſt, that we uſe hoſpitality;'

having ſung which, ſhe wiped the long peſtle, and
placed it again where it had been before, and cleaned
off the aſhes from her head and arms.

" No longer able to refrain from aſking the meaning of ſuch a ſingular act of devotion, the *Pandaram*
ſaid, ' Never have I beheld ſuch a marvellous *Poojei*
as this. The rice-peſtle is to ſeparate the huſks from
the grain; and I have heard two women, when ſtand-
ing oppoſite each other handling their rice-beaters,
and preſſing them down upon the *paddi* in front of
them, ſing as they proceeded with their work; but
you, madam, have performed a *Poojei*, and what kind
of worſhip this is I ſhould much like to know.'

"' It is a *Poojei*,' replied the merchant's wife,
' which is peculiar to the deity of our caſte, and is
only performed by women when they meet with a
ſtranger;' then, in an undertone, intended for him
to hear, though uttered as if ſpeaking to herſelf, ſhe
added, ' All in good time, my good *Pandaram;* you
will find out faſt enough what kind of a ſacrifice this
is when you enter the houſe and it is completed on
the crown of your head.' Then, reſuming her former
bland tone of welcome, ſhe ſaid, ' Had you not better
walk into the houſe, ſir? The hour of tiffin draws

nigh, and my hufband will be here in a trice. Pray follow me;' and taking up the rice-beater in both her arms, fhe led the way into the houfe.

" But the *Pandaram*, imagining nothing lefs than that he was to be made a facrifice to the deity of the cafte to which the *chitty* belonged, no fooner faw her enter, than, looking upon difcretion as the better part of valour, he took to his heels, and rufhing at all fpeed through the gate of the court, never looked behind him till he found himfelf fafely enfconced in a little alley leading out of the ftreet.

"In the meantime the merchant had reached home, and not finding the *Pandaram* as he expected, 'What now, huffey!' faid he; 'where is the gueft whom I fent home to abide my return from the bazaar?' 'A pretty fort of gueft, forfooth,' fhe replied; 'furely he was not himfelf, or he muft have been mad. No fooner had he entered, and I had fpread the mat on the bench for him, than, fpying the rice-peftles, he defired me to give him one of them; and upon my faying that you would foon be home, when he could make the requeft to you, as without your authority I could not give it to him, he took himfelf off in a huff, muttering fome ftrange words to himfelf, which I could in no way underftand.'

" 'Woman,' rejoined the *chitty*, 'would you bring ruin upon me and upon my houfe? Once for all, let it be clearly underftood, that whatever any holy *Pandaram* may afk, you have my full and per-feet permiffion to give to him. Quick, give me the rice-beater, that I may follow him, and thus, even by the tardy gift, avert, if poffible, the evil which may otherwife befall us;' faying which, he took up the rice-peftle, which fhe handed to him, and rufhing into the ftreet, fpied the *Pandaram* crouched up the alley on the oppofite fide of the ftreet in which he had taken refuge.

"' *Pandaram! Pandaram!*' fhouted the *chitty*; when the holy man, feeing the merchant approach him with the rice-beater in his arms, took again to his heels, faying to himfelf, 'Surely, furely, he is about to complete the *Poojei* on my head;' and the thought made him redouble his fpeed, till he had completely diftanced the good *chitty*, who, ftanding high in the eftimation of his fellow-citizens, and feafting daily upon all the good things of this life, as rich citizens are wont to do, was fat and purfy, and foon had to give up the chafe for want of breath. The ftory of the rice-beater *Poojei* foon got bruited about amongft the holy brotherhood, and the mer-chant, do what he would, after that could never per-fuade a *Pandaram* again to darken his doors. So his young and pretty wife obtained the object fhe had in view; and even if the merchant did not obtain his by the means he had intended, it was not long before he deferved a cufhion, and liftened fondly to the prattle of a fon and heir.

"Now, fir, this is rice-beater *Poojei;* and if you

will let me perform it on the rear of that fniggering *Poorahita,* it will transfer the fulfilment of his prophecy from your perfon to his, turning the chill of which you complain into heat, and giving you a frefh and firm hold on life for many years to come."

Upon this the Gooroo Simple could not help burfting into a loud laugh. "Of a truth," faid he, "it is not without caufe that men call you *Afangadan* and Merriman; for however ferious may be the fubject which engroffes the attention, you have always a joke to crack or a tale to tell."

Seeing that his tale had had the defired effect upon his old friend, Merriman, cafting afide all banter, and fpeaking ferioufly, replied, "My dear Gooroo, the words of the *Poorahita* are no doubt words of truth, and cold is in the rear when death is near; and the *Oodfameiyams* with their inner light, and the *Poorrachchameiyans* with their outer, can both explain why death is not near when there is cold in the rear, though there muft be cold in the rear when death is near. Let us analyze carefully the cabaliftic words, and fo obtain their true meaning, which can have no reference to the chill occafioned by extraneous caufes. You fell into the ditch, and, fitting in the cold water, *afanam fhitam* followed as a natural confequence, which common fenfe and friction, without even the application of the rice-beater *Poojei,* fhould have changed into heat; for what is there wonderful in the rear of a man becoming chilled who fits up to his middle shivering in cold water? The wonder would be all the other way; and the *jivana nasham* need not trouble you, who can so readily account for the *asanam shitam* of yesterday. Test what I say by applying the warmth of the fire or the heat of the sun to the place affected. Be of good cheer, and banish from your mind all fear and dread, and in future only then believe the *jivana nasham* at hand when, without sitting down in the mire, or falling into the water, or without any other extraneous cause, you find the *asanam shitam* already there. Believe me, sir, any other view of the case is absurd; all nonsense, and worthy only of the father* of Somasarman, the moon's own; so true it is that "they who seek wisdom only from books, without a knowledge of the ways of the world, are but learned fools, and reap the world's contempt.'"

When a man can laugh, Dharma's spell is already broken; and the Gooroo's laugh had been both loud and hearty, when Merriman had concluded his story of the rice-beater *Poojei;* so he continued to listen attentively to the deductions the latter had just made clear, and having eaten nothing since his unsavoury bath of the day before, he found a gnawing in his inside, which fully convinced him that his friend was right, and that the *asanam shitam* he had experienced had nothing to do with the *jivana nasham* he had dreaded, so he ordered the preparations for his

---

* Sfabhafakripana (one miserable through his own folly).

fepulture to be put afide, and breakfaft to be ferved inftead. In a few days he went about as ufual, vifiting his flock as formerly, and edifying the people by obferving all the rites and *poojeis* of the cafte to which he belonged, as heretofore, in the moft exemplary manner.

So things went on pleafantly till the rainy feason had fet in; when one night, after he had retired to his bed, a perfect hurricane of wind and rain broke over the mattam, and as that part of the roof under which the Gooroo flept was fomewhat dilapidated, the rain came pouring in upon the old man; but fo foundly did he fleep, that neither wet nor cold fufficed to break his flumbers. Towards morning he turned from one fide to the other, refting with his back upon that part of the mat upon which he flept, which had become fully faturated by the wet. Suddenly waking up, and feeling the chill at his rear, he lay for fome time confidering whence it could have its rife, faying to himfelf, " I have not been fitting down in the mire, neither have I fallen into the water, and here, within the mattam, there cannot be any extraneous caufe for this damp chill which has feized upon my rear. Of a truth,"—it was his favourite expreffion—" now is the fulfilment of the prophecy of the Brahman at hand. This damp chill is the cold perfpiration of death. It is needlefs, then, to wreftle with Dharma."

Hereupon, when Noodle, Doodle, Wifeacre, Zany, and Foozle came in with the breakfaft, he told them that now the time was come when he would have to depart from them; "that as the *afanam fhitam* was caufed by no extraneous circumftance, the *jirana nafham* muft follow as a matter of courfe." Unfortunately, Merriman was not in the village at the time, to have difabufed his mind of this new folly, and his difciples were no lefs perfuaded than himfelf as to the abfence of all extraneous caufe for the chill that had fo fuddenly feized upon the part, and therefore readily coincided in the view which he had taken, that what the *Poorahita* had foretold was now about to come to pafs. The people of his cafte, too, who came to vifit him, being poffeffed of no more fenfe than his difciples, faw much wifdom in the deductions he had drawn, and all coincided with the words he groaned out in his diftrefs of mind, that "now beyond all doubt the fulfilment of the prophecy was at hand."

He continued in this defponding ftate for feveral days, refufing all food, and not allowing any converfation to divert his mind from the one abforbing thought of death and the grave, till excitement and want of fleep and fuftenance brought on delirium, in which he lay for three days, uttering without ceafing, "Cold in the rear when death is near." Completely exhaufted, he at length fell into a fwoon, upon which his difciples, believing him dead, rent the air with their lamentations, placing their hands upon their heads, howling, weeping, and crying out, "He is dead! the great and good Gooroo Simple is dead!

Our beloved mafter is dead! He is dead!" And thus they continued to fhout as they performed all the preliminary ceremonies of preparing the dead for fepulture, which, being completed, they next proceeded to the purification of the body by immerfing it entirely in water.

Now for this purpofe it was neceffary that it fhould he carried to a large trough, which ftood in the outer court of the mattam; fo whilft Foozle went and filled the trough up to the brim with water, Wifeacre and Noodle, Zany and Doodle, raifed up the Gooroo from the mat upon which they had laid him out, and carried him to it, each crying all the way, with a loud voice, " He is dead! he is dead!" and immerged him into it, Wifeacre and Noodle holding him down with might and main by the hands and feet, whilft Doodle, Zany, and Foozle, rubbed and ferubbed with all their might, to purify the corpfe for fepulture.

This rubbing and ferubbing brought the lethargic blood of the old man again into circulation; but being under water, he could not open his mouth to fpeak, and when he tried to free his hands and feet from the grafp of Wifeacre and Noodle, they, believing that fome demon had taken poffeffion of the body of their beloved mafter, only held him down firmer in the water, till, overcome in the ftruggle, nature gave way, and the Gooroo perifhed thus miferably from the ignorance of his difciples.

This ftruggle over, the body remained cold and

paffive in their hands. Having dried it and perfumed it, they placed it in a fitting pofture on a litter, adorned with flowers, and threw open the gates of the mattam, when the villagers came thronging in from all the places belonging to his circuit, to do honour to the dead. Then his difciples lifted up the body, Noodle and Doodle, Wifeacre and Zany fupporting it on either fide, whilft Foozle preceded it in front, and the villagers followed in the rear, and as they placed him in the grave and buried him, they chanted folemnly the myftic words:

ASANAM · SHITAM · JIVANA · NASHAM .

NOTES,

ILLUSTRATIONS,

AND

GLOSSARY.

A · PENNYWORTH · OF · MIRTH · IS · WORTH
A · POUND · OF · SORROW.

NOTES AND ILLUSTRATIONS.

INTRODUCTION.

PAGE 17.—The fables which with the Englifh reader pafs as the productions of Æfop are of various periods and of various countries; but as epic poetry was a perfect infpiration when it ftarted into being in the Iliad and Odyffey, no lefs so was the Μῦθος, or Fable, of the Phrygian; and later mythologifts have only approached, but never equalled, the great original. The Wolf and the Lamb, the Mountain in Labour, the Belly and the Limbs, the Fox and the Stork, the Boys and the Frogs, all belonging to the earlieft period, are ftill unfurpaffed. If we compare thefe fables with thofe which are attributed to Pilpay or Bidpay, including thofe found in the two Pantfhatantra, the texts of which have been made acceffible to us, that of the South in the French paraphrafe of M. Dubois, publifhed at Paris in 1826, and by means of Englifh tranflations of the Hitopadefa, and the other in the German verfion of Prof. Benfey, which appeared at Leipzig in 1859, we cannot fail to recognife the truth of this remark.

It is cuftomary to place fome three hundred years between the productions of Æfop and Pilpay, affigning to the former the date of 550 B.C. as the period when he flourifhed, and to the latter 250 B.C.; but thefe

M

dates are at best uncertain. Indeed, as with Homer, several countries contest the honour of the birth of the former; Lydia, the Island of Samos, Thrace, and Phrygia, being all mentioned as his native land by authors entitled to our consideration, though, on the authority of Phædrus, Lucian, Aulus Gellius, and Stobæus, it has become general to ascribe that honour to the last. Following Diogenes Laertius, in his Life of Chilo, the date of Æsop's Fables has been fixed at the period just stated.

It may not be out of place to mention that the great fabulist was not the deformed being he is represented. That deformity was first attributed to him by a Greek monk in the fourteenth century. Planudes, as is well known, confounded the Phrygian sage with the early oriental fabulist Lokman, who is described as "deformed, of a black complexion, with thick lips and splay feet." Indeed, Planudes, not content with distorting the person of Æsop, palmed off many of his own crude compositions as the fables of the latter; but these are easily detected, as he makes use of words and sentiments after the style of Scripture, rather than following that of pagan writers, and introduces manners, and quotations from authors, of much more recent times. Prof. Benfey, in speaking of the fables in the Pantshatantra, says that most of them, more or less, are reproductions of those of the West, particularly of those which belong to the period of Æsop, though, as some of them are unmistakably of Eastern origin, he inclines to the belief that this class of literature may have been cultivated in India even prior to the introduction of Æfop's Fables, and marks this diftinction between them, that the Greek fabulift embodies the natural inftincts of the animal in the words placed in its mouth, whilft the Oriental writer merely clothes the human foul with the animal's form, originating in the Indian belief in the tranf-migration of fouls.

PAGE 20.—Prof. Benfey traces the origin of the Pant-fhatantra to Buddhifm, and, as fhown at pp. 29—35 of our Introduction, the fatire in that work is levelled equally unfparingly againft the Brahmans, as is that in thefe Adventures of the Gooroo Paramartan.

PAGE 26.—Tamul literature confifts chiefly of medi-cal works, written by thefe Poorrachchameiyans; of works on philology*; grammar being, according to Prof. Benfey, an early creation of the Buddhifts; of hiftories of the Chola, Pandya, and Chera kingdoms; and of dramatic, didactic, and moral poems, the latter, almoft exclufively, the productions of Valloovan Pariars. In the feventh volume of the *Afiatic Refearches*, Dr. John gave a life of Avyar, a female writer, with trans-lations of feveral of her poems, and Mr. Ellis com-menced printing at Madras the text of the celebrated *Kurral*, or *Cooral*, of Tiroovalloovan, the Divine Valloo-van, whofe name is ftill unknown, the moft celebrated of thefe moral poets, the following aphorifms from which have been introduced into our text :—1. " Home and its comforts are ours, but in truft to exercife hof-pitality ;" page 162. 2. " Is not virtue the greateft gain, and its neglect the greateft lofs ?" page 131. 3. " There muft be a beginning ; even as A is the firft letter of the alphabet, fo is God the beginning of the Univerfe;" page 132. 4. "The world is within him who underftands the way of five things—of tafte, of light (*i. e.* of *fight*), of touch, of found, of fmell;" page 128. 5. "Sweet is the lute to them, who know not the found of their children's prattle;" page 109. 6. "They who reach the feet of Him, who nourifheth the opening flower, fhall flourifh;" page 114. 7. "Be humble, be courteous. Without thefe of what avail are other qualities?" page 130. And 8. "Life may yet be his who has obliterated all other virtues, but from him who has blotted out the remembrance of benefits received, life has furely departed;" page 132. Of Mr. Ellis's edition, which is accompanied by a tranflation, and an analyfis of each diftich, 777 pages have been printed, embracing the beft portion of the firft twelve chapters, and it is mentioned with much commendation by Mr. Anderfon, in the preface to his *Tamul Grammar,* publifhed in 1821, and no lefs fo by Mr. Babington, in his edition of *The Adventures of the Gooroo Paramartan.* Unfortunately, this book is not acceffible; but extracts from the Kurral will be found in Kindersley's *Specimens of Hindoo Literature,* and in Wilfon's *Defcriptive Catalogue of the Library of Colonel Mackenzie,* vol. i. page 233.

The grammatical treatifes are, no doubt, the ground work of the Shen and Koden Tamul Grammars of Father Befchi, the latter of which was publifhed in 1738, under the title of *Grammatica Latino-Tamulica de Vulgari Tamulicæ Linguæ Idiomate.* The former ftill exifts in Latin, only in manufcript, but a tranflation of it was publifhed by Mr. Babington, at Madras, in 1822, as *A Grammar of the High Dialeƈt of the Tamil Language, termed Shen-Tamil. To which is added an Introduƈtion to Tamil Poetry.*

Many of the hiftorical treatifes in Tamul were col-leƈted and printed at Madras, in 1835, by Mr. Taylor, in two volumes quarto, under the title of *Oriental Hiftorical Manufcripts in the Tamul Language.* Be-fides thefe original works, Tamul literature has been much enriched by tranflations and imitations from the Sanskrit, including a verfion of the Pantfhatantra. The title runs thus :—*Pancha Tantra Katha : Stories trans-lated into the Tamul Language by Tandariga Muda-liyar.* It was printed at Calcutta in 1826. Manu-fcripts of the Pantfhatantra of early date exift in Tamul, and M. Dubois, fpeaking of the fources of his French paraphrafe, fays, " Le choix que nous publions a été extrait fur trois copies différentes, écrites, l'une en Tamul, l'autre en Telougou, et la troifième en Can-nada."

PAGE 28.—In the text of our paraphrafe the fol-lowing aphorifms from the Pantfhatantra, fimilar to that printed in Italics, have been introduced :—1. " What is ordained for him will fall to the lot of man. Even the gods cannot hinder it. Therefore, do not let us repine at fate, but wonder; for that which is ours belongs to none other;" page 41. 2. " A prudent man trufts to a true friend in the day of trouble, for no one overcomes adverfity without a friend;" page 106. 3. " No, not upon mother or wife, brother, or even upon one's own son, can a man fo firmly repofe as upon the boſom of a tried friend ;" page 106. 4. "Without money even the brighteſt intellect will be absorbed and deſtroyed by carking care for butter and ſalt, for oil and rice, for raiment and wood ;" page 120. 5. "They who ſeek wiſdom only from books, without a knowledge of the ways of the world, are but learned fools, and reap the world's contempt ;" page 170.

The reader who is curious in the Pantſhatantra literature will find an admirable *Analytical Account of the Pancha Tantra*, by Mr. H. H. Wilson, in the *Tranſactions of the Royal Aſiatic Society*, vol. i. p. 155, etc. In Dr. Graeſſe's "Tréſor des Livres rares et précieux," under Bidpay, is a liſt of editions of the Pantſhatantra, and of the portion known as the Hitopadeſa, which figured in the infancy of printing under the Latin title of *Directorium Humanæ Vitæ*, a copy of which was ſold for £31 10s. at Sir Mark Sykes's ſale. But the ſtudent ſhould not omit to conſult Prof. Benfey's admirable eſſay on the ſubject, to which he has already been referred, if he wiſhes fully to maſter the ſubject in all its bearings.

PAGE 31.—Kajakuddſha (Kanodſha) is the Kanoje of our maps, the Kanyacubja of the Hindoos. According to Feriſhta it was formerly the capital of a kingdom, and from the mention of it in the text of the Pantſhatantra as a place of education, it was probably alſo a college, ſimilar to that of Madura, which was eſtabliſhed by the native princes. It is ſuppoſed to be the Calinpaxa of Pliny, and Hindoo ruins extend round it for ſeveral miles, but its chief public buildings at prefent only confift of the citadel, tombs, mofques, and other Mohammedan edifices.

PAGE 35.—Befides the aphorifms from the Kurral and from the Pantfhatantra, already noticed, the Hebrew proverb, תרי קבי רחמרי הר קבא דקיטייתא וסריח:, has been put into the mouth of the Gooroo at page 130; and from our own vernacular fayings the following will be found in the text:—1. "The longer the faw of grief is drawn the hotter it grows;" page 54. 2. "Fools and their money are foon parted;" page 55. 3. "He that has but one hog makes him fat; and he that has but one tale to tell never comes to the end of it; for he that cannot hold his tongue muft have leave to fpeak;" page 59. 4. "Like lips, like lettuce;" page 60. 5. "Bleffed be the memory of him who invented fleep;" page 68. 6. The Roman fatirift's "Rem, recte fi poffis, fi non, quocunque modo rem;" page 119. 7. "Hope is the waking man's dream; it is a good breakfaft, but a bad fupper;" page 128. 8. In my own city my name, in a ftrange city my clothes, procure me refpect;" page 132. 9. "In the coldeft flint there is hot fire, and there is life in a mufcle; and while there is life there is hope;" page 143. 10. "If thou haft increafed thy water, thou muft alfo increafe thy meal;" page 155. 11. "A cheerful mind, peace, and fimple diet are the beft medicines;" page 159. 12. "Who goes to bed fupperlefs fhall tumble and tofs;" page 159. The other aphorifms are all part of the Tamul text.

The manners and cuftoms of the Tamuls, which are incidentally illuftrated in the preceding page, are not the leaft attractive portion of the work, which, confining itfelf chiefly to fatire on the Brahmans, neverthelefs gives us a glimpfe of various other fects, more particularly by bringing the Gooroo and his difciples into immediate contact with Pariars, or Outcafts from the four orthodox cafes of Brahmans, Kfhatriyas, Vaifyas, and Sudras, mentioning the literary Valloovans, and the scientific Poorrachchameiyans and Oodsameiyans. Of the former of thefe laft-mentioned Father Befchi records in his MS. Dictionary, quoted by Mr. Babington, that they form "Six fectes exterieures, dont la premiere eft peu connue, la feconde eft fecte de Buddha, la troisième aujourd'hui fort odieufe (c'eft de cette fecte que font fortis la plupart des livres de Sciences), la quatrième auffi peu connue, la cinquième, fecte de la cinquième nuit, parceque, lors qu'il y a cinq vendredis à un mois, ils celebrent la nuit du cinquième avec de grandes abominations, et la fixième, fecte des phantafliques qui n'admettent rien de réel, excepté peut-être Dieu." The *Oodfameiyams* he calls " Secte interieure, c'eft a dire qui place dans le corps humain les lettres mifterieufes, *na, ma, ka, va,* et *ya.*" There are fix fects of *Oodsameiyams,* as well as of *Poorrachchameiyans.*

We have alfo the Tamul computation of time :— 1. The four ages of the world, as mentioned at pages 119, 141, 206. 2. The divifion of the year, at page 188. 3. The divifion of the day, at page 187. 4. Lucky and unlucky days, at page 111 ; and 5. The periods of woman's life, at page 211. Then, too, we are introduced to the interior and duties of the mattam at

pages 38, 60, 64, 69, and 72; and its Poojeis and
worship, at pages 70 and 209; its kitchen and
cookery at page 70 and 72; its cleanlinefs at page 60;
and the perfonal ablutions and clothing of its inmates
at pages 70, 97, 192, and 207.

We are alfo fhown the ufes of the village choultry
(temple, court of juftice, and inn all in one) at pages
87—95, and at page 118; and get an infight into the
functions of the native rural magiftracy at pages 89—
95, and page 123, with judgments, if not rivalling
thofe of the great governor of Barataria, at leaft
only fecond to them; of fuperftitions and belief in
magic arts at pages 39, 55, 124, and 160; of exhibi-
tions of fpite and ill-will at pages 53, 147, and 152; of
grief and lamentation at pages 53 and 172; of notions
of riches and pleafure at page 109; of piety and good
works, at pages 97 and 193; and of reafoning and forethought at page 101; all of which are as graphically
portrayed as if they had been fketched by the Barber
of the Arabian Tales himfelf.

THE FIRST STORY.

PAGE 37. The proper duty of a *Brahman* is to
teach the *Vedas*, to perform facrifices to the gods,
and to meditate upon divine and holy objects. At
an early age he is placed under the inftruction of a
Brahman called a *Gooroo*, whofe commands he is
bound to obey, and whom he muft reverence as a
fpiritual teacher. For an account of the office of
Gooroo, fee *Dubois's Mœurs, Inftitutions, et Céré-
monies des Peuples de l'Inde.* Thefe priefts hold

the first rank amongst the Brahmans. In the Deccan many of them possess an authority which bears some resemblance to that of a suffragan or diocesan bishop in the Christian Church, being placed over a district, and having jurisdiction in everything relating to religion and caste. They travel in great state, a satire upon which is furnished in the fifth story in the present volume, where the Gooroo Simple sets out on horseback from the house of the peasant who gave him the old worn-out horse; and they receive large contributions from their disciples. See the article "Hindustan," in the *Penny Cyclopædia*, in which, quoting from *Buchanan's Journey in the Mysore*, it is stated that "the Rajah of Tanjore is said to give his Gooroo daily two hundred and fifty pagodas (about £92) when that personage honours him with a visit." According to the strict letter of the law, a Brahman ought to be supported by the rich, and not to be obliged to gain his subsistence by any laborious or useful occupation. Failing this, the *Institutes of Menu* (x. 81, 82) permit him to become a soldier, to follow trade, to till the land, or to breed cattle. Many of the Sepoys in the late Anglo-Indian army belonged to this caste.

In the original Tamul the name of our Gooroo is *Paramartan*, "simple, without guile." It seemed a pity to adopt the name given to him in Mr. Babington's literal translation of the text, particularly as *Noodle* is the English equivalent to *Pedei*, the name of one of the young Brahmans, which he has rendered Simpleton; so we have rendered it

Simple. *Matti* (blockhead), *Madeiyam* (idiot), *Pedei* (simpleton), *Mileichan* (dunce), and *Moodan* (fool), are exactly reprefented by our Englifh words, *Wifeacre, Zany, Noodle, Doodle,* and *Foozle.*

PAGE 38.—The *Mattam* is the cell of the *Gooroo,* in importance fimilar to one of our fmall religious houfes before the period of their fuppreffion under Henry the Eighth, in which that fpiritual inftructor exercifes all the functions of his calling as prieft and teacher, and in which are contained the temple, refectory, dormitories, audience-chamber, &c., the whole forming the refidence of the Gooroo and the young Brahmans under his charge. The Brahmans poffefs the exclufive privilege of teaching the *Vedas,* and were in former times the fole depofitaries of all knowledge. According to *Bohlen's Altes Indien,* though the rulers were chofen from the cafte of *Kfhatriya,* or Warriors, the Brahmans poffeffed the real power, and were, as we find by the *Infiitutes of Menu* (viii. 1, 9, 11), the royal councillors, the judges, and magiftrates of the country. They were treated by fovereigns with the greateft refpect; for, according to the fame authority (ix. 313—317), "a Brahman, whether learned or ignorant, is a powerful divinity." His curfe could even confign the gods to mifery, inftances of which are given in the *Mahábhárata,* the great epic poem of the Hindoos.

The Tamuls divide the twenty-four hours into eight watches, each confifting of three hours, four for the day, and four for the night, fo that the third watch is mid-day.

PAGE 39.—According to old Tavernier, the brand carried by Tamul travellers is "un ligne entortillé et trempé dans l'huile que l'on met dans une manière de rechaud au bout d'un baton," a hint from which our smokers may profit.

PAGE 43.—The year is divided into six parts, each consisting of two months, and the Tamul month begins about the middle of our own. The first period is the *rainy season*, August and September; the second, the *cold season*, October and November; the third, *the first dew*, and the fourth, the *latter dew* (expressions which recal the words in *Deuteronomy* xi. 14), embracing respectively December and January, February and March; the fifth, *the hot season*, April and May; and the sixth, *the hottest season*, June and July. The year consists of twelve lunar months, and to make up for the extra days, the Tamuls add every three years an intercalary month of thirty days. The first day of their new year answers to our twelfth of August. The month of the vernal equinox, from the earliest ages of antiquity, from the usages of Babylon and Assyria, is still preserved throughout the East. See the two volumes published by the Society for the Diffusion of Useful Knowledge, under the title of "*Hindoos*."

PAGE 44.—The fable of the Dog and the Shadow is due, perhaps, to Æsop or Socrates, to the latter of whom we probably owe the collection which now passes under the name of the Phrygian. Its type, however, is found in some of the earlier collections of the East, and in Benfey's *Pantschatantra, fünf*

Bücher Indiſcher Fabeln, aus dem Sanſkrit überſetzt
(vol. i. p. 79), the queſtion as to its oriental origin
is fully diſcuſſed. M. Dubois was at firſt inclined
to believe it to have been introduced by Father
Beſchi, but he changed his opinion, and adds,
" mais je n'ai pas tardé à changer de ſentiment,
et j'ai connu bientot que cette fable était originaire-
ment indienne, et généralement connue dans le pays."
However, the curious reader is further referred to
Benfey's *Pantſchatantra*, vol. i. *Einleitung*, pp. 468,
9, where the fable of the Jackal and the Fiſh is given
as the probable ſource of the more beautiful Greek
embodiment of graſping greed. In our text, as in the
Æſopian fable, deceived by the magnifying power of
the water, the dog miſtakes the ſhadow for a larger
joint, which makes it not improbable that Beſchi may
have inſerted it, probably borrowing it from Poſſinus's
Latin text of the fable.

PAGE 50.—In the Tamul text the noiſeleſs ſtep into
the water is repreſented "as if it were *jala-jala*," and the
preſſing the foot downwards, " as if it were *too-nookoo*,"
giving this ſound of the water by the expreſſions uſed,
both natural words, coined for the occaſion.

PAGE 51.—The reader may probably recollect a
ſimilar circumſtance, as narrated in the tenth of the
Merry Tales of the Wiſe Men of Gotham. Mr.
Babington ſuggeſts that Beſchi may have borrowed it
from that tale; but as it is not very likely that he had
acceſs to the book, it ſeems, on the contrary, more
probable that, being of oriental origin, it ſhould, like
many ſimilar tales in the *Geſta Romanorum*, the *Owl-*

glass and other collections, have found its way gradually from the East to us in the West. The English tale runs thus :—

"On a certain time there were twelve men of Gotham that went to fish, and some stood on dry land; and in going home one said to the other, ' We have ventured wonderfully in wading; I pray God that none of us come home to be drowned.' ' Nay, marry,' said one to the other, ' let us see that, for there did twelve of us come out.' Then they told themselves, and every one told eleven; said the one to the other, ' there is one of us drowned.' They went back to the brook where they had been fishing, and sought up and down for him that was wanting, making great lamentation. A courtier coming by, asked what it was they sought for, and why they were sorrowful? ' O,' said they, ' this day we went to fish in the brook; twelve of us came out together, and one is drowned.' Said the courtier, ' Tell how many there be of you.' One of them said ' eleven,' and he did not tell himself. ' Well,' said the courtier, ' what will you give me, and I will find the twelfth man?' ' Sir,' said they, ' all the money we have got.' ' Give me the money,' said the courtier, and began with the first, and gave him a stroke over the shoulders with his whip, which made him groan, saying, ' Here is one,' and so served them all, and they all groaned at the matter. When he came to the last, he paid him well, saying, ' Here is the twelfth man.' ' God's blessing on thy heart,' said they, ' for thus finding our dear brother.'"

PAGE 53.—"The Hindoos," says Mr. Babington, "in uttering a malediction, unite their hands by interlacing the fingers, and then, projecting them forwards, produce the sound commonly called cracking the joints. Their imprecations are still further strengthened, as they think, by casting dust at the object of them."

STORY THE SECOND.

PAGE 60.—" C'est de cette manière que les maisons des Indiens sont purifiées des souillures qui peuvent y avoir été imprimées par les allons et les venans." See Dubois' *Mœurs de l'Inde*, vol. i. page 208. The cow is held sacred by the Hindoos; and even the Sikhs, who reject the authority of the *Vedas, Puranas*, and other religious books of the Hindoos, and eat all kinds of flesh except that of the cow, hold that animal in great veneration. Penances of a singular and severe nature were formerly enjoined for killing cows without malice, and if this crime was maliciously committed, it admitted of no expiation whatever.

PAGE 62.—The original gives the number of women as *ten*; but the numerals *ten* and *four*, in Tamul, are employed to give a definite idea of an indefinite number, the same as in Homer *nine* is applied in regard to time : ἐννῆμαρ μεν ἀνὰ στρατον ὤκετο κῆλα Θεοιο.

PAGE 70.—" Toutes ces pratiques," remarks M. Dubois on this passage, " et un grand nombre d'autres encore, sont usitées et font partie de la bonne éducation parmi les Indiens." According to Mr. Babington, the ablutions and cleanlinefs enjoined by the law, in conformity to Hindoo practice, confiſt in four particulars: 1. Shaving, which is performed on every part of the body, excepting the top of the head, the upper lip, the arm from the elbow to the wriſt, and the leg from the knee to the ankle (the Brahmans, however, fhave the upper lip). 2. Anointment, or, according to others, the bathing of the whole body, as oppoſed to a bathing or wafhing of the head as far as the neck. 3. Care and cleanſing of the teeth. And 4. Clean raiment. The author of *Hindoſtan in Miniature*, fpeaking of Malabar barbers, obſerves, "They commonly fet up fhop under a tree, the foliage of which fcreens them from the fun. Their bafin is the half of a cocoa-nut fhell, and their razors have very broad blades, the edge of which is convex;" vol. v. 35.

Poojei, worfhip, fee note at page 210.

PAGE 72.—*Cucurbita Hiſpida*, afh-coloured pumpkin.

PAGE 73.—The *kadam*, fomething like our word mile, is a meaſure of diſtance varying in different parts of India. At Madras and in Tamul countries it equals ten Englifh miles.

PAGE 74.—The following is fuggeſted as the origin of the phrafe to chaff a perſon, our flang term for making game of any one. Apollo received from a painſtaking critic a volume filled with the errors of the great poets. By way of reward for fuch bootlefs labour, the god of poetry gave him a bufhel of wheat to fort, bidding him to feleƈt the corn from the chaff.

When this was done, Apollo prefented the critic with the chaff, but retained the wheat, thus *chaffing* him, and making game of him. See *Boccalini's Adver-tifements from Parnaffus*, a favourite book with Addifon.

PAGE 75.—Two Tamul aphorifms: *They who per-form penance are forwarding their own affairs;* and *From pious actions alone proceeds delight; all elfe is irrelevant and unworthy of praife.* "The Tamul," fays Mr. Babington, "reckon thirty-two kinds of pious actions, fome of which are fufficiently fanciful; thefe comprehend, however, if not all the poffible varieties of charitable works, at leaft more than moft people perform. Their enumeration is as follows:—1. The building hofpitals for the poor. 2. Giving food to thofe whofe employment is devotion. 3. Giving food to thofe who follow any of the fix feets. 4. Supplying calendars or almanacks. 5. Furnifhing remedies for the eyes. 6. Giving oil for the anoint-ment of the head. 7. Affociating with the female fex. 8. Marriage. 9. Sobriety. 10. Preferving the good works of another. 11. Raifing a fhed where water may be furnifhed gratis to travellers. 12. Building a houfe either of reft for travellers, or for fome religious devotee. 13. Building tanks and re-pairing roads. 14. Planting trees. 15. Planting groves for the convenience of travellers. 16. Giving food to animals. 17. Giving money to preferve the life of any living thing whatfoever. 18. Erecting pofts for cows to rub themfelves againft. 19. Giving food to prifoners or flaves. 20. Giving boiled rice for

N

facrifices.   21. Caufing to make facrifices.   22. Giving garments.   23. Furnifhing provifions for a journey.
24. Furnifhing Brahmans with the means of bearing
the expenfe of affuming the facred thread.   25. Pouring milk into the facrificial fire.   26. Making gifts,
more efpecially of money.   27. Giving quick lime, to
be eaten with betel leaf.   28. Paying for the barber
employed in fhaving another.   29. Furnifhing remedies for difeafes.   30. Giving drink to cows.   31. Furnifhing a looking-glafs.   32. Burning corpfes."   For
an explanation of the nature and value of thefe various
good works, the reader is referred to Rhode's *Religiöfe
Bildung, Mythologie und Philofophie der Hindus.*

*If you fow a cafter-oil tree, will an ebony tree be
produced?* is an old Tamul aphorifm which cannot
fail to remind the reader of the words in the Sermon
on the Mount, *Matthew* vii. 16.

PAGE 79.—This "Counting the chickens before
they are hatched" is to be met with in the folk's
lore of every language, in fome fhape or another, the
well-known ftory of the Day-dreamer in the *Arabian
Nights* being of courfe familiar to every one, no lefs than
the old adage, "*Ante victoriam, ne canas triumphum.*"
Dreamland, if geographers would but be honeft, would
be found to cover a far larger portion of the globe
than we like to admit, and not confine itfelf to
Spain and its caftles; but, perhaps, rather, as in the
cafe of the Schildbürgers, the natives having, in their
folly, deftroyed their own city, have, like the Jews,
become a fcattered race, and are met with in every
inhabited country.   The mention of the Schildbürgers

recalls a tale from the *Lalenbuch*, edited by Von der Hagen in 1811, from which the ſaying of "Counting the chickens before they are hatched" may have had its riſe; as the date of the *Schildbürger*, the original type of our *Wiſe Men of Gotham*, is placed at the beginning of the thirteenth century, the period at which the ſpread of the Mogul Empire into the Weſt brought with it the Mooriſh verſions of many Eaſtern tales, to be ſpeedily engrafted into the literature of the Weſt. It forms the thirty-third ſtory in the *Lalenbuch*, and runs thus:—

"*How a Woman of Schilda went to Market with Eggs, and made much Account of what Good would come of the Produce; and what really did come of it.*

"There is an old proverb and a true, which ſays, 'Sell not the bear's ſkin before you have caught him;' and another, no leſs ſo, tells us that 'Covetouſneſs brings nothing home;' whilſt a third adds:

> 'To hope, when hope is long deferred,
> Makes many a fool, it is averred;
> Before the hoſt to name the ſcore
> But ſeldom adds to one's own ſtore.'

This was the caſe with the woman of Schilda, who went to market with her eggs, as you ſhall ſee. Now this poor woman had but a ſingle hen, which laid an egg every day; ſo ſhe gathered them up till ſhe ſaid to herſelf, 'Now I have enough to bring me

three groschens!' when, putting them into a basket,
she set off to market with them. As she had no
companion to talk to as she trudged along, all kinds
of thoughts got into her head, and, amongst others,
she naturally reverted to her little stock-in-trade, which
she carried jauntily upon it, thus turning it to a pro-
fitable account:—' See now,' said she, to herself, ' you
will get three groschens at the market. What will
will you do with them? Do with them? Why, buy
two more hens, to be sure. These two, with the one
you have at home, in so many days will lay so many
eggs, which, when sold, will enable you to buy three
more hens, and leave a lot of profit besides. Therefore, now, as you have six hens, they will lay so many
eggs every month. These you will sell—now and
then, however, you may eat one yourself—and you
may put all the money by. Then, too, you will
derive profit from these hens in various ways. The
old ones, when they have done laying, you will turn
into money; the young ones will lay eggs, and hatch
some of them into chickens, and so you will increase
your stock at the same time that you have also
chickens to sell; then you can pluck their feathers,
like people do geese. Out of the money you have
put by you will buy some geese, and these will bring
you much profit by the sale of their eggs, their young,
and their feathers. Now, as you have both hens and
geese, your profits will amount weekly to so and so.
Then you will purchase a she-goat; she will give you
milk, and little kids. Thus you have already old and
young hens, old and young geese, eggs, feathers,

milk, kids, and wool—of courfe you will fee to have the goat fheared. Then you will purchafe a fow, and, to your former profits, you will thus add fucking pigs, pork, hams, and faufages. All this will enable you to buy a cow out of the money you are always laying by. She will produce milk, calves, and manure. What is the good of the manure to you, feeing that you have got no land to till? To be fure, you will purchafe a field, and that will yield you corn, fo that you need not buy any more. Then you will buy fome horfes, and hire farm-labourers to look after them, to milk the cows, and till the land. Next, you will buy a flock of fheep, when you will want to enlarge your houfe, and to furnifh it out of the money you have laid by. After which you will purchafe more land. Now, this cannot fail to come about. So, then, you will derive profit from young and old poultry and hens; from eggs, from goat's milk, wool, and young kids; from lambs and fucking pigs; from cows, whofe horns you may alfo have fawed off, and fell to the cutler for knife-handles; from calves, from corn-fields, and many other things befides. And, laft of all, you will marry a young and handfome man, and be a fine lady, as happy as the day is long. Oh, fo grand! and not have a good word for any one! "A tafte of the falt, but not of the malt," is the peafant's motto, and their coat of arms, three fingers in the falt-cellar; but that fhall not be ours, forfooth.'

" ' Whilft thefe thoughts ran in her head, fhe forgot that fhe was only then trudging to market with the basket upon it; so, drawing one leg behind the other, she bent her head gracefully forward, as if a fine lady, greeting another she had met, when, lo! down went the basket, and smash went the eggs, and, with them, 'My lady!' and 'My lord!' into the mire; and there they remain to this day; and if any one is so inclined, he may pick her up, and become a lord with such a lady; for 'it is a long time before you can count your chickens from unlaid eggs.' "

The tale of *The Broken Jar*, in the fifth book of the Pantshatantra, is no doubt the source of this story of the Woman of Schilda.

"The man with the wheel said, 'Every man who is influenced by a futile hope, as by an evil spirit, is an object of ridicule.' Therefore it is wisely written :— *'He who indulges in silly projects for the future, deserves to fare as did the father of Somasarman, who was smothered in rice till he became white.'*

"The alchemist asked, 'How was that?' Then the man with the wheel told the story of

The Broken Jar.

"In a certain town there lived a Brahman, whose name was Svabhavakripana,* who filled a jar with what remained of the boiled rice he had collected during the day, after he had satisfied his hunger, and hung it up by a string low down on a nail in the wall. This done, he placed the mat upon which he slept beneath it, and all night long he kept his eyes fixed upon

* One miserable through his own folly.

the jar, thus thinking within himſelf: 'That jar is
brimful of boiled rice ; now, if a famine ſhould come,
it will bring me a hundred fanams. With them I
will buy a couple of goats; and, as theſe multiply
every ſix months, I ſhall ſoon have many kids and a
whole herd of goats. Theſe I will exchange for
beeves. Then I ſhall have many calves in due time,
which I ſhall ſell; and after a while I will exchange
the increaſed herd of beeves for buffaloes. After they
have brought forth their increaſe, I will part with
them for brood-mares; and when the foals have become horſes I ſhall ſell them, and ſo become poſſeſſed
of much money. With this money I will purchaſe a
houſe, the four ſides of which are built round an inner
court. Then a Brahman will come and give me a
fair damſel with great dower for a wife. She will
bring me a ſon, to whom I will give the name of
Somaſarman ;* and when he is old enough to climb
up my knees, I will take a book and ſit down in the
ſtables and ſtudy. When Somaſarman ſpies me out,
he will tear himſelf away from his mother's lap, and
ruſh in amongſt the horſes' hoofs in his hurry to come
and climb up my knees. Then, full of anger, I ſhall
call out to his mother, 'Take the child away ! Take
the child away !' She, being fully occupied with her
houſework, does not hear me ; upon which I ſpring
forward and ſtrike out my foot at her.' Forgetful, at
the moment, that he was lying down on his mat, he
ſtruck out with his foot with ſuch force that he broke

* Cared for by the Moon, or the Moon's own.

the jar into shivers, and the rice came running down upon him till it completely covered him and made him white. That is why I said, ' He who indulges in silly projects for the future deserves to fare as did the father of Somasarman, who was smothered in rice till he became white.' "

Respecting the origin of all oriental tantra or tales themselves, we are probably on the eve of a great discovery. Dr. David Chwolfon, who is professor of Hebrew in the University of St. Peterfburg, has recently issued a very curious and interesting volume* on the remains of ancient Babylonian literature in Arabic translations. According to it, a person named Kuthami compiled a well-planned and ably-executed work on general literature fourteen centuries before the Christian era, giving us glimpses of a previous civilization of some three thousand years. We are promised the Arabic texts, accompanied by a translation. When these appear we shall have more certain data than mere conjectural criticism for fixing dates. Kuthami, it seems, speaks of " the ancients," the writers of periods then long passed away, as we do of the authors of classical antiquity.

PAGE 82.—A finger's breadth is the common measure, equivalent to our inch.

---

* Ueber die Ueberrefte der Alt-Babylonifchen Literatur en Arabifchen Ueberfetzungen. Von D. Chwolfon. St. Peterfburg, 1859.

STORY THE THIRD.

PAGE 85.—*Paffoun-kircy*, a plant, of which the stalk, always pendant and dry, gives it the appearance of being dead.

PAGE 91.—A bundle or clothful of boiled rice is the usual viaticum of an Indian journey. Moderate in his appetites, the Hindoo is satisfied if he can impart a relish to it by a little pepper-water, or the juice of a lime, or any other simple condiment. In many instances such is also the home breakfast; for rice is used in great profusion by the Hindoos, who mostly sit crofs-legged on a cushion, mat, or carpet at meals, helping themselves from the dish in the most primitive form with their hands, having neither knives nor forks, and difpenfing generally with the use of a table-cloth. The univerfal dinner dish is curry, confisting of meat or fish, and dressed in various ways.

PAGE 90.—The *Choultry* in villages serves many purpofes; it is the temple, the hall of jufice, the place of meeting, the lodging for travellers, and, in fome places, also the tavern, where ready-dressed provifions may be obtained. The kitchen in the latter cafe is also the refectory. See Dubois's *Mœurs de l'Inde*, vol. i. p. 458.

PAGE 92.—The *Darma-Saftra*, or *Dharma-Saftra*, is a celebrated body of Ethics, Law, and Ritual Ob-fervances.

The Francifcan, Thomas Murner, has appropriated

both incidents of this story in the seventy-eighth adventure of Eulenspiegel, or Owl-glass, as given in our recent edition of Mr. Mackenzie's English version. See *The Marvellous Adventures and Rare Conceits of Majier Tyll Owl-glass*, p. 180.

STORY THE FOURTH.

PAGE 97.—The Tamuls are very delicate in all references to such matters : " To seek the privacy of the fields, to go for a purpose, to go for two purposes, to go to the bath, to go to the river, to go out," &c., are the usual expressions. In the original the passage reads : "*Whilst they were refreshing themselves there, Wifeacre retired to the fields, and then went to wash his feet in the neighbouring tank*," the " washing of the feet " implying the prescribed ablution of the body, in consequence of his previous " private visit to the fields."

Ayinar, the son of Vishnoo, carries a club, and rides upon a white elephant, his banner displaying a cock.

PAGE 102.—This story is somewhat similar to that told of the Wise Men of Gotham, who raked in a pond for the moon, which the reader will find in the *Merrie Tales*.

PAGE 106.—*Kasoo* is the Tamul word, but it is mostly pronounced *cashoo*, or simply *cash* by Europeans, and though only the eightieth part of a *fanam* it is also used as we do the word *cash*. *Fanam*, as well as being the designation of a coin, is equivalent to the word money, just as *peny* is used by our translators of the Bible. It is a silver coin, of which forty-five go to a ftar pagoda. There are alfo gold *fanams* in fome parts of India; but Befchi ufes the word in all cafes without diftinguifhing whether gold or filver, leaving the reader to judge from the article to be paid for—whether a horfe, the toll on the road, or the pounding of the worn-out animal upon which the Gooroo journeyed—which coin is meant.

STORY THE FIFTH.

PAGE 109.—*Ghee* is equivalent to our word *mefs*, a mefs of pottage, of meat, &c.; and like the Latin *ferculum*, means the principal difh of the meal. *Tyer* is a folid curd, fuch as is eaten in Germany with boiled fruit, &c., and is produced by the addition of a fmall quantity of milk already curdled to the milk intended to be changed to *tyer*. In India it is ufually eaten with rice.

PAGE 120.—In the beginning of the thirteenth century Zingis, or Gengis Khan, founded the immenfe empire of the Moguls, comprehending almoft the whole of Afia, and a great part of the Eaft of Europe. The tenth map in Spruner's Hiftorico-Geographical Atlas fhows this empire in its entirety, before it was feparated into different kingdoms.

We have here the well-known ftory of Vefpafian and Titus. When the latter remonftrated with Vefpafian upon the meannefs of laying a tax on urine, that emperor, taking a piece of money, demanded if the fmell offended him? adding, that this very money was the produce of the tax on urine. It is, no doubt, an in-

terpolation of Befchi, and, as fuch, has been omitted
by M. Dubois. However, it was thought better to
retain it in the Englifh paraphrafe, as it forms part of
the printed Tamul text. The reader will recollect the
allufion to it by Juvenal : *" Lucri bonus eſt odor ex re
qualibet."*

PAGE 124.—The *Valloovan* is a prieſt of the
Pariars, and confequently confidered vile by the
orthodox caſtes. Thefe prieſts have gradations of rank
amongſt themſelves, and many of them follow con-
juring and fortune-telling. See Dubois's *Mœurs de
l'Inde*, vol. I. page 68. Almoſt all the moral poems
in Tamul are written by the *Pariars*, the moſt celebrated of which is the Kurral of *Tiroo-Valloovan*, or
the Divine Valloovan, as already ſtated.

The outcaſts are called either *Pariars*, or *Chan-
dalas*, and in diſtricts where both words are employed,
the *Chandala* is the loweſt of all *Pariars*, and is only
employed to carry out corpſes, execute criminals, and
in all the moſt abject offices to which a human being
can be condemned. The *Pariars* confiſt of all who
have loſt caſte, or by their mifconduct have forfeited
all the privileges of it. Their condition is the loweſt
degradation of human nature, and hence it is not to
be wondered at, that the Hindoos fo refolutely adhere
to the inſtitutions of their tribe, becaufe the loſs of
caſte is to them the loſs of all human comfort and
refpectability. If a *Pariar* approached a *Nayr*, a
warrior of high caſte, he might put him to death with
impunity ; and water and milk, according to *Ayeen
Akberry* (vol. III. p. 243), are confidered defiled even

by the shadow of a *Pariar* passing over them, and cannot be used till they are purified.

STORY THE SIXTH.

PAGE 130.—In the original text the passage runs: " Ah! even the grain of fine rice is within its husk, and to fruits of every kind there are a skin and a stone." The Tamuls no not include nuts, plantains, and shell-fruit, under the general denomination of fruit, as we do, which would render the more literal translation a little obscure in English.

PAGE 133.—In one of the plates of Hogarth's *Contested Election*, there is a man seated at the ex-tremity of the sign-post of the Crown Inn, sawing off the portion on which he rests. No one will charge our pictorial satirist with plagiarism, and the circum-stance is only mentioned to show how certain ludicrous ideas are common all over the world. The same idea occurs in various early Sanskrit authors, and is con-tained in an anecdote related of *Kalidasa*.

PAGE 134.—*Poorahita*, or more properly *Poorohita*, is the name given to Brahmans who devote themselves to the study of astrology, and who preside at festivals and other ceremonies. See Dubois's *Mœurs de l'Inde*, vol. I. p. 180.

PAGE 136.—*Shafter*, *Shastah*, or *Sastra*, is the name of a sacred book of the Hindoos, containing all the dogmas of the religion of the Brahmans, and all the ceremonies of their worship, and serving as a com-mentary on the Vedas. This name is also applied to any book of great wisdom, as in the third story we find mention of the *Dharma-Shajtra*. It likewise signifies wisdom, or a wise man, whence *Buddha* is also called pre-eminently *Shajiri*, in the sense that Wise-acre applies the word to the *Poorohita*. Indeed, it is a title often assumed by the Brahmans, sometimes with the suffix of *Sahib*, *Shaftri-Sahib*, Mr. Shaftri. The word *Shajier* is used in the eighth story by the Gooroo, as tantamount to " a true or wise saying."

Am! am! ma! Dear, dear me! Prodigious! wonderful! the common exclamation of great wonder and admiration throughout India, perhaps derived from the mystic syllable used previous to prayer, *Oum!*

Namascara : " C'est ainsi qu'on appelle le salut adressi aux Brahmes : ce salut se fait en joignant les mains, les portant au front, et inclinant en même temps la téte."—*Dubois.*

PAGE 139. *Aservahdam*, congé, dismissal.

Baron Munchausen may have borrowed this idea. See page 139 of our edition of his *Surprising Adventures*, where the lunar language of Central Africa is found to be " identical with that of the inhabitants of the Moon."

PAGE 141.—YOOGAM in Tamul, *Jogue* in Hindostannee, is an age of the world, of which there are four, according to Hindoo reckoning. 1. The *Sooti-yoogam*, which lasted 3,200,000 years, during which the life of man was 100,000 years, and his stature twenty-one cubits. 2. The *Tirtah-yoogam*, which consisted of 2,400,000 years, during which man's life was 10,000 years, and in which one-third of the human race lapfed into fin. 3. The *Dwapaar-yoo-gam*, which endured 600,000 years, during which human life was reduced to 1000 years, and half the race became depraved. And 4. *Kali-yoogam*, in which fin is univerfal, human life diminifhed to 100 years, and which is to laft 400,000 years, of which fome 5000 are already paft.

STORY THE SEVENTH.

PAGE 144.—The roads in India are not unfrequently lined with banian trees, each one of itfelf a grove, forming natural fhady bowers, impervious even to an Indian fun, as from the horizontal branches pendant roots hang downwards, which, upon reaching the ground, become new trunks.

PAGE 147.—*Tchy! tchy!* Fie! fie! a common exclamation of extreme difguft. "Ceux qui favant vivre, ne difent jamais ce mot devant les perfonnes de diftinction, ni hors du difcours familier."—Befchi's *MS. Dictionary,* quoted by Mr. Babington.

PAGE 148.—*Cadjan,* a prepared leaf of the palm tree, upon which the Tamuls cut in the letters with a ftile. In the Britifh Mufeum, and at the Eaft India Mufeum, are many of thefe manufcripts, both Tamul and Pali, which of late years have become comparatively common in the fhops of European bookfellers who deal in oriental literature.

PAGE 151.—Mr. Babington furnifhes the following interefting particulars refpecting the drefs of the Tamuls, both male and female:—"The articles of clothing among the Tamuls are few and simple, though their names, some of which are synonymous, and others expressive of differences in manufacture, colour, and other circumstances, are extremely numerous. It seems probable that anciently they wore no sewn garments, and that the jackets now so much in use among the higher classes of citizens, and the bodices worn by dancing women as well as by females of the higher orders, were introduced by the Mussulmans on their conquest of the country. To this day, those who, residing far from towns, and following rural occupations, are less disturbed in their observance of the customs of their ancestors, wear none but long, unsewn cloths, in the precise state in which they come from the loom; and in none of the ancient sculptures of Southern India are either jackets or bodices to be found, the men or gods being represented naked, and the women being furnished with a broad ornamented belt, which passes horizontally across the breasts and under the arms. The turban is likewise of modern introduction and partial use. The Brahmans, with the exception of those who hold official situations, seldom wear it; and many other classes, more especially in the country, go bareheaded, even in the hottest weather. The genuine dress of the men, therefore, consists of—1. a cloth round the loins, which delicacy absolutely demands, and which is the only covering worn by the labouring classes; 2. a cloth of 8 cubits in length, which is passed several times around the waist and between the legs, thus entirely covering the lower half of the perfon; 3. a cloth of four cubits' length, which is ufually carried over one of the fhoulders, and is occafionally ufed to cover the head; and 4. a cloth of from 19 to 20 cubits, which envelopes the upper part of the perfon. Perhaps the fhort trowfers, reaching half way down the thighs, and worn by foldiers and athletes, may be alfo of ancient origin. To thefe we may annex the modern additions of the turban, of 30 cubits' length; the linen veft, which fits the body in the upper part, and has a full fkirt; and the trowfers worn by dancers."

The true drefs of the women is a fingle cloth of 14 cubits in length. By dexterity in the art of wrapping this around the waift, and bringing the end over the fhoulder, the females of India form as elegant and modeft a drefs as that made with fo much labour, and adjufted with fo much art, by the fair fex in Europe.

The ufe of the needle and fciffors, therefore, which fome feem fo anxious at the prefent time to teach them, would prove at beft but a needlefs art. It might even be morally hurtful, becaufe thofe additional articles of clothing which require to be made up are principally ufed by courtefans and thofe whofe fubfiftence depends on decoration of perfon. There were, befides, an under bodice, and loofe drawers or trowfers."

STORY THE EIGHTH.

PAGE 161.—*Poojei*, worship, act of devotion, penance; Anglo-Indians often spell the word *pooja*. At page 70 Doodle gives an insight into the ceremonial of Hindoo worship, which consists in decorating, anointing, and making offerings to the idol. Sacred music accompanies this ceremony, the officiating Brahmans chanting hymns to the deity, whilst dancing girls propitiate his favour by a solemn dance.

PAGE 162.—*Chitty*, a merchant. The Brahmans hold that of the four castes, *Brahmana*, Brahmans; *Kshatriya*, Warriors; *Vaisya*, Merchants, and *Sudra*, Cultivators, only the first and last remain in the present *Kaliyoogam*, or last age of the world. Those, however, who hereditarily follow commerce maintain that such is not the fact, and that they are true and genuine merchants. There are three distinct occupations allotted to this general caste: trade, agricultural labour, and rearing of cattle; all of which a Brahman may also follow.

Pandarams, religious mendicants of the sect of Siva, the third person in the Hindoo *trimurti*, or triad of deity. The *Saivas*, or worshippers of *Siva*, are more numerous than any other sect. Respecting Hindoo mythology consult Coleman's *Mythology of the Hindoos*; and Rhode's *Religiöse Bildung, Mythologie, und Philosophie der Hindus*.

PAGE 163.—In the original it is "a young wife

whom he had bought." Moft Hindoo marriages are contracted by the parents when the parties are in childhood, and the wedding is folemnized with great pomp when the children reach maturity. A woman brings no other fortune than her clothes and orna- ments, and two or three female flaves, and the father of the bridegroom frequently pays a fum of money to the bride's friends. Hence the terms, "He has married a wife," and "He has purchafed a wife," are ufed quite as fynonymes.

The females are noted for delicacy, regularity of features, and extreme modefty; they are marriage- able at the age of eleven years, and are accounted old at forty-one. The Tamuls divide the natural life of woman into feven ages, fix of which are prior to forty-one, at which age fhe receives a title fome- what refembling our "old crone."

Charity and hofpitality are not idle words amongft the Hindoos. "Hofpitality," according to the Infti- tutes of Menu, "is to be exercifed even towards an enemy when he cometh into thy houfe; for the tree doth not withdraw its fhade even from the woodman, nor the moon withhold her light from the out- caft *Chandala*."* The latter paffage cannot fail to recall the words of the Sermon on the Mount (*Mat- thew* v. 45.) "Les riches idolâtres," fays the old traveller Tavernier, "s'eftiment heureux et croyent

* The word *Chandala* is here ufed to denote the vileft of the *Pariars*. It is alfo applied to children of mixed marriages, where the mother is of the Brahmana, and the father of the Sudra cafte.

que leur maifons font remplies des benedictions du
Ciel, lorfqu'ils ont pour hôtes quelques-uns de ces
Faquirs, qu'ils honorent d'autant plus qu'ils font plus
d'aufteritez."

PAGE 165.—" On each fide of the door towards the
ftreet is a narrow gallery covered by the flope of the
roof which projects over it, and which, as far as the
gallery extends, is fupported by pillars of brick or wood.
This entrance leads into a court, which is alfo furrounded by a gallery like the former.   On one side of
the court is a large room, on a level with the floor of
the gallery, open in front, and fpread with mats and
carpets covered with white cotton cloth, where the
mafter of the houfe receives vifitors and tranfacts
bufinefs.   From this court there are entrances by very
fmall doors to the private apartments."—*Hindoftan in
Miniature*, vol. viii. p. 518.

PAGE 165.—The rice-beater is ufed by the Tamul
women to deprive the rice of its hufk, and is a kind
of peftle, or long ftaff, made of fome hard wood,
moftly ebony, and fhod with metal.   The *Paddi*, as
the rice is called whilft in the hufk, is collected into a
heap upon a hard floor, or fometimes into an excava-
tion in the ground.

" Two women ufually work together," fays Mr.
Babington, " oppofite to one another, with the
heap between them, and each receives and raifes
the inftrument with the left hand, and then forces it
down again violently with the right, giving it a
flight inclination forwards, fo that it may eafily be

caught by the left hand of the oppofite party. As the rice becomes difperfed, it is pufhed back into the centre with the left foot, caufing a graceful fide movement; whence refults a conftant though flow revolution around the heap. This work, as indeed every other kind in India, which is performed by more than one perfon, and admits of adaptation to mufical meafure, is accompanied by a fong."

Mr. Babington fuggefts this rice-beating procefs as an illuftration of *Proverbs* xxvii. 22. The hand-mills of India are ftill fuch as thofe defcribed in the Bible, at which two women may frequently be feen grinding, as mentioned in *Matthew* xxiv. 41. The *Saivas*, of whom the chitty's wife was one, place three horizontal lines on the forehead with afhes, obtained, if poffible, from the hearth on which a confecrated fire is perpetually kept.

PAGE 167.—The word *huffey* muft be here taken in its better fenfe of wife or houfewife. The pet name for a woman is *Am*, literally the bafe or foot of a thing, but ufed alfo to exprefs admiration (fee Note at page 206). However, it is only ufed, lovingly, by a hufband to his wife, by a father to his daughter, or by a fon to his mother, or by women amongft themfelves, and is confidered indecorous when coming from an indifferent perfon.

PAGE 172.—This placing of the hands upon the head to denote great grief and affliction is the cuftom alluded to in 2 *Samuel* xiii. 19, and in *Jeremiah* ii. 37.

" Cette pratique de laver les cadavres avant de les
enterrer ou de les brûler, est univerfellement fuivie
par les Indiens de toutes les caftes."—*Dubois.* In
fome parts of India, after thefe ablutions have taken
place, the body of a prieft is embalmed with the
coftlieft fpices procurable, and placed in a cheft filled
with honey, when it is put away for the day of public
fepulture, or the funeral pyre, generally months after-
wards.

Arrived at the place, attended by immenfe num-
bers of people who form the proceffion, and met
by others from all the furrounding diftricts, two
parties feize upon the car, one at either fide, and
commence the ceremony of " caring," by tugging at
it with all their might, the one reprefenting thofe
who defire to inter the body, and the other thofe who
would commit it to the flames. Whichever is fucceff-
ful carries the point, and the body is either buried or
burned accordingly. A feene of wilder tumult and
excitement cannot well be conceived than what takes
place at one of thefe funerals, at which all kinds of
revelry and vice prevail, and which tend only to
bring together the people for their own demoral-
ization.

The *Poojei* over, the honey, which has been carefully put by when the body was removed from the
cheft, is bottled, and finds its way into the Calcutta
market, and hence, with the delicacies of European
cookery and Indian preferves, to the tables of our
epicures.

After all, it is with manners and cuſtoms as with everything elſe ; ſo let everybody join in the ſtrain :—

ASINUS · ASINO · SUS · SUI · PULCHER ·

ET · SUUM · CUIQUE · PULCHRUM ·

ERRATA · SIC · CORRIGE.

P. 20. Gaudama *pro* Guadama.

P. 24. Malayalam *pro* Malayatam.

P. 35. *et semper lege:* Poorohita.

P. 170. Svabhavakripana, v. *pro* f.

A.

ACHEDANAMOORTI, irrational, 159.

AM, foot, bafe of a thing, pet name for a woman, dear, 206.

AM-AM-MA, dear, dear me, wonderful, prodigious, 136, 206, 213.

AMOORDAM, the drink of the gods, 118.

ASANGADAN, a mocker, merriman, 26, 159, 169.

ASSIRVAHDAM, congé, difmiffal, 139.

AVOOR, a town in Trichinopoly, 21.

AVYAR, a Tamul poetefs, 179.

AYINAR, the fon of Viſhnoo, 97, 202.

F.

FANAM, a gold or ſilver coin, money, 55, 58, 87, 93, 94, 118, 124, 202.

FAQUIR, a religious mendicant, 211.

Fo ol ſand the irm one ya refo onpar ted, a mere tranſpoſition of the Engliſh adage, Fools and their money are ſoon parted, 55.

G.

GAUDAMA, the apoſtle of Buddhiſm, 20.

GHEE, meſs, diſh, ſimilar to the Latin *ferculum*, 109, 203.

GOOROO, firſt rank of Brahmans, ſpiritual guide, teacher, 22, 32, 36, 70, 115, 185, 187.

H.

HEM, ſo, an exclamation, 30, 31, 51, 80, 130.

HINDOO, or Gentoo, 18, 19, 25, 26, 27, 37.

J.

JALA-JALA, plop-plop, 50.

K.

KADAM, mile, equal to ten Engliſh miles, 73, 192.

KALIYOOGAM, the fourth and laſt age of the world, 114, 141, 207.

KANJAKUDDSHA, the town of *Kanoje*, 32, 182.

KASOO, or Kaſhoo, a ſmall coin, caſh, 129, 202.

KSHATRIYA, the warrior caſte, 25, 184, 187, 210.

KURRAL, a celebrated poem, conſiſting of above thirteen hundred moral diſtichs, by the Tiroovalloovan, 179, 180.

KUTHAMI, an ancient Babylonian author, 200.

M.

MADEIYAM, idiot, 187.

MADURA, a college eſtabliſhed by the Tamul princes, 182.

MAHABHARATA, the celebrated Hindoo Epic, 187.

MATTAM, the Gooroo's cell or convent, 38, 58, 60, 65, 71, 156, 171, 184, 187.

MATTI, blockhead, 187.

MENU, the compiler of Inſtitutes of Hindoo Law, 187.

MILEICHAN, dunce, 187.

MOGUL, foreigner, the Tartar ruler of India, 19.

MOODAN, fool, 187.

MURDHABHISHICTA, a Brahmanical ſect, 25.

N.

NAMASCARA, mode of ſaluting a Brahman, 136, 139, 206.

NAYR, a ſoldier of high caſte, 204.

O.

OODSAMEIYAMS, name of ſix ſects, 162, 169; deſcribed, 184.

P.

R.

S.

SASTRA, SHASTRI, SHASTER, a sacred book of the Hindoos; wisdom; any book of great authority; a wise man, a prophet, a true and wise saying, 93, 94, 136, 141, 157, 205.

SIKHS, a warlike people of India, who reject the authority of the *Vedas*, *Puranas*, and other books of the Hindoos, 191.

SIVA, or Shivan, the third person in the Hindoo triad of deity, 162, 210.

SOMA, the Moon, 170.

SOMASARMAN, in the care of the Moon, 170, 198.

SOOTI-YOOGAM, the first age of the world, 141, 206.

SUDRA, the caste of cultivators, 25, 184, 210.

SVABHAVAKRIPANA, through one's own folly miserable, 170, 198.

T.

TAMUL, a primitive language, spoken by the inhabitants of Southern India, etc., 21, 22, 24, 180. Literature, 179—182.

TCHY, fie, 147, 207.

TEMBAVANI, a Tamul poem, by Befchi, 22.

TIROO, divine, 179.

TIRTAH-YOOGAM, the second age of the world, 141, 206.

TOONOOKOO, plafh-plafh, 50.

TYER, curds, 109, 159.

V.

VAIDYA, a Brahmanical sect, 26.

VAISYA, the merchant caste, 25, 116, 184, 210.

VALKEER, a breeder of cattle, 33.

VALLOOVAN, a priest of the *Pariars*, 26, 27, 124, 132, 179, 184.

VEDAS, the most sacred books of the Hindoos, 25, 185, 187, 191.

VIRAMAMOONI, the Jesuit Beschi, 21, 49, 50.

VISHNOO, the second person in the Hindoo triad of deity, 97, 202.

Y.

YOOGAM, a period of the world's age, 141.

Z.

ZINGIS, Gengis Khan, 120, 203.

THE END.

LONDON:

WILLIAM STEVENS, PRINTER, 37, BELL YARD,
TEMPLE BAR.

www.ingramcontent.com/pod-product-compliance
Lightning Source LLC
Chambersburg PA
CBHW022002050726
47498CB00007BA/2564